VENDETTA

A MAFIA ROMANCE

VENDETTA

A MAFIA ROMANCE

ELLIE SANDERS

CONTENT WARNING

Please skip this page if you do not want a warning.

This is my twist on the Medusa myth. It's not a retelling. As one would expect with such a story, there are triggers. Hints of rape, but no explicit telling. There's violence, explicit sex, including a lot of public sexual activity. There's also murder, torture, I mean it's one hell of a ride if you're willing to take a punt.

But be aware this book is not for the faint hearted. Please read at your own discretion. This is an 'adult' novel for a reason.

*Medusa; They raped her when she was beautiful
and they killed her when she was ugly.*

Her

Preface

The first cut is the worst. The second is almost as bad. I can feel my skin splitting, my blood pouring out, covering me.
I scream but it doesn't make any difference. It doesn't make them stop.

My hands are behind me. Held behind me. I'm unable to fight. Unable to defend myself. Someone rips at my clothes and I vaguely register the freezing air hitting my skin.

Another blow comes, this time it hits me in the side of my head and it rattles inside me, making my very brain shake. I can feel someone touching me, groping me. I fight again, or at least make an attempt to and they laugh at the pitifulness of it.

I'm a joke to them. A laughing stock. My pain, my utter terror is a source of amusement to these men, to these rabid animals.

I try to wriggle free and the hands holding me let me fall hard into the disgusting stench of the alleyway that they dragged me into. My face slams into the concrete and I feel the rainy water soaked ground leech into what little clothes I have left.

I roll over, my breath catching in my chest and I stare up at them with my eye which isn't swollen shut.

And they stare back. They laugh. I don't even know them. Not properly. Not really. But apparently they know me. They've been watching me they say. Admiring me for nights on end.

They stand over me, their shadows covering me and I know I'm trembling, shaking, petrified of their next move.

I've pissed myself. I can smell the stench of it, the stench of my own acrid urine. It fills my nostrils. It mixes with the iron taste of my blood.

One of them laughs nudging me with his boot.

If I'd given in, if I'd let them fuck me willingly then perhaps I wouldn't have ended up like this. At least that's what they're saying. That this is my fault. I deserve this. I shouldn't dress the way I do. I shouldn't walk the way I do. Look the way I do too.

I glance at my torn off clothes. Jeans and a t-shirt are hardly the clothes someone wears when they want attention but apparently I was asking for it.

"Stupid bitch." One of them says grabbing my hair and wrenching my head up.

I spit at him and it lands right in his face making him snarl.

He pulls a bottle of something, gives it a shake and pours it over my face as I scream once more.

The liquid burns even as I try to get it off. I can feel it searing into my skin, melting my very flesh. I curl up. Contort. I'm in agony as I shriek louder and louder and they stand there, watching, laughing again.

I can't see. I can't think. I thought the pain of their knives was enough but this new torture is something else entirely.

As the darkness takes over, as the agony of each horrific millisecond gives way to unconscious I see them running. Fleeing. Someone new is approaching. Another stranger. Another man I don't know.

Only I'm too broken to fight now.

He pours more liquid onto me and I whimper but it doesn't burn like the last time. It almost soothes.

And then he picks me, cradles me, and as he carries me away I give in.

I give up.

I surrender.

Him

CHAPTER
One

I've been watching her all night.

Though she acts unaware I know that she knows. A girl like that isn't stupid. A girl like that isn't oblivious. The scars on her face, the scars on her body tell me that.

She walks, no, glides about the space. Her body still beautiful, still wanton, despite the obvious trauma.

Her hair is down. Just like always. And the curves I know she has, are hidden under the overly baggy shirt.

Preston watches her too. Just for a second before his eyes flit to the other women. The other barmaids.

In a line up, none of my men would pick Eleri. None of them would give her a second glance. They'd see the scars, they'd see the way she holds herself, no, hides herself and they'd choose one of the others. The world has brought them up to want an Instagram worthy, filter perfect image of a woman. A plastic fantastic model with perfect eyebrows, perfect lips, and a size zero body to boot.

And all the other girls try to adhere to this ridiculous ideal as if it were gospel.

But Eleri, Eleri is different. Eleri is perfect.

Two men in the corner knock over a glass and the beer splashes everywhere. Eleri is quick to respond grabbing a cloth and moving to catch the liquid before it spreads too far.

I watch as she bends over, as she gets on her knees and dabs the floor at these men's feet. One of them murmurs something and the other smirks before he looks at her properly. And then the smirk on his lips drops.

He sees the scar concealed by her hair. He sees the way her skin is marked and his face reacts in disgust.

Eleri sees it too but she doesn't say anything. She doesn't even respond. She just continues doing her job. Doing what all my other god damn staff should be doing except they're flirting right now, flirting with my men, oblivious to anything in the hopes that they might score the bigtime.

You see that's what they're all here for. That's why they work at my bar. It's not that the pay's good, although it's not bad. It's not that it's glamourous. My club is where the glamour is at but this bar is where I reside most often.

And that's why they want to work here.

It's because of who I am. And who my associates are and the life one of us could raise them to.

That is, everyone except Eleri, because she works here for me. Though she doesn't know it yet. She doesn't have a clue.

I've spent the last two years stalking this woman, watching from the shadows, playing her guardian angel and manipulating everything around her till I was ready to make my move. Till she was ready too.

And now I can feel that we're finally at this juncture.

I nod my head at the doorman and he reacts instantly signalling to everyone else to get the fuck out. It's late anyway, past last orders, but we don't play the rules here. We make our own rules.

As I lean back in my seat one of the barmaids walks up with a glass of whiskey. Neat. Just how I like it. She places it on the table in front of me and then sits down, leaning forward enough for me to get a good view of her tits beneath the curve of her tight top.

I look. It would be rude not to and then I meet her eyes. Her lips are curled. She's smiling just enough to be enchanting.

"Go away." I say and her eyes widen as her face falls.

She gets up quickly. Thankfully she has enough brains not to push anything further.

Preston stares at her ass as she walks away. She's making a point of swinging her hips, sashaying them, as if her body could compare with the girl now hiding in the corner. Hiding in the shadows.

"You need to learn to play nice." Preston says and I laugh.

"No thanks." I say back. I don't play nice. I have no reason to. Niceties are for fools. For weaklings. I play to win. And I always do.

Preston gets up and leaves me to it. Clearly he wants to play with the barmaids and I'm more than happy for him to. He's a big boy. He can occupy his own space for a while.

My eyes flit to Eleri once more. I could wait. I could leave it another night but my skin is itching and I'm done waiting. Hell I've waited two years already. Two long, agonising years.

She makes the mistake of looking at me. Just for a moment. Her head turns enough that our eyes meet and I know then that the moment is now. She's made the decision for me. She's sealed our fate.

I beckon her to me and as she takes each slow step I see the briefest litany of emotions cascade across her face. And then the mask comes down.

My fierce beauty. My defiant snow queen becomes a statue. A perfectly unreadable stranger.

"Sit." I say quietly.

The music is still playing but it's quiet enough for her to hear me. I see her throat move, the only evidence of her nervousness now but she does what I tell her. She is obedient.

I flex my hands, unseen under the table. I'm itching to see how obedient she can be. To push her. To really test her but she's not ready and I won't rush her. At least not yet. Softly softly, catch a beauty.

She drops her gaze, keeping her focus on the amber nectar in front of me and I take the moment to study her.

It's been a while since I've seen her face properly. It's changed so much. Evolved. The low lights bounce off her skin, illuminating the scarring as if she were a painting. She must be wearing makeup, foundation at least to hide the redness of her skin. The thought irritates me. That she feels the need to conceal herself. To hide herself. But the way the t-shirt hides her body shows that she wants to be anonymous. Unnoticeable. A nobody.

Only my little ice queen can never be that. She will never be that.

Because I notice her. I see her. And I refuse to let her hide now.

She's breathing slowly. Calmly. I look around at the few other people nearby. Preston is busy chatting up the same girl I sent running.

But Eleri looks cool as a cucumber. As if she isn't even here. As if her she's zoned out. Her hair hangs thick over her shoulders and I want to yank on it so hard, to force her into giving some sort of reaction that I almost do it.

"Look at me." I say and she does. Again without hesitation.

Her beautiful doe eye meets mine and for a moment I think I might be lost in that look. She frowns for a moment and I take the opportunity to sip my whiskey.

She is nervous. She's skittish. Behind the façade. Behind the calm exterior this girl is like a rocket threatening to go off. I see her leg jerk for a second and I wonder if she might just flee.

"Do I scare you?" I ask her.

She nods.

I'm not surprised. Almost everyone in this city is scared of me. Or at least the smart ones are.

"What if I promise not to hurt you?" I say.

She shakes her head slightly.

"Speak. Tell me what you're thinking."

I don't believe such promises." She says.

I smirk. "Are you calling me a liar?"

"No." She replies not looking fazed. "But most men make promises they easily break."

"I am not most men." I state but mentally I file that comment away, beyond her attack I wonder what other ways she's been betrayed, what other ways men have chosen to hurt her.

She blinks. That's all the reaction I get. The audacity of this girl is outstanding. Perhaps that's why I want her. Why I need her.

"Can I go?" She says quietly.

I grind my teeth. On the one hand I could play nice, lull her in softly, like an injured animal, build her trust if you will but I don't think it would work and I don't have the patience for such games.

"Do you know why you work here?" I ask letting her hear the edge to my voice, looking at the vein pulsing in her neck, spiking with her adrenaline.

She nods. She works here because my bar is the only place that will employ her. None of the fancy hotels would have a girl with her face on show. None of the other bars would want her. It's here or the streets and we both know she won't choose that. Besides, I've made sure she has no other options. Any other place that might hire her was told not to under no uncertain terms

17

because I wanted her here. I needed her here. She has to be under my watch. Where I can see her. Where I can study her.

"This is my bar. I own it."

"You don't own me." She says but her face reacts. Her blood drains and I see she thinks she's made a mistake.

"Oh Eleri." I murmur and her face falls more. She didn't think I knew her name. She just assumed she was a nobody to all of us. A ghost almost. "I will own you." I say. "I will own every part of you."

She gets up, half stumbles from the stool and my men look round at the sudden movement. I lift my hand slightly to tell them to stay where they are. I won't have them touch her. I won't have anyone touch her.

"I am not yours." She says but she's trembling. Falling apart.

I want to hold her, to feel as her body crumbles within my grasp, but I don't. I just watch as her fear takes over.

"Don't fight me Eleri." I say narrowing my eyes. But in truth I want her to. I want to see what spirit she has. I want to unleash the monster I know resides in her. That's why I chose her. That's why I stalked her.

She is no ordinary girl. The scars, the trauma attests to that.

But she's not a victim either. She's a fighter. My fighter. And I want to see how much damage she can do.

CHAPTER

Two

I run out of the bar.

My heart is thumping. My adrenaline is coursing through me. I feel like my whole body is on fire. Aflame. And not in a good way.

I don't know why he's decided now of all days to make a move but I know already that I won't escape this. Won't escape him.

He's been watching me too long. Stalking me almost.

For over six months I've worked at this bar. The only one that would have me. My face means every other place has literally shut the door on me. Slammed it shut.

My only other option would be the streets and after what happened two years ago I wouldn't resort to that if my life depended upon it.

Besides no one would want someone like me. No one can even look at me without wincing so why would they pay money to fuck me?

At yet he wants me.

Nico Morelli. The mob king himself.

I gulp at the thought. My pace has slowed. My feet are stilling.

I'm in an alleyway. Not the same as the one I was attacked in but it's so familiar it sends a chill through me.

It's late or early depending on how you look at it. If there wasn't so much light pollution there would be stars above my head.

As the smoke, and the semi-darkness, and the stench of the something rotting fills my nostrils I feel myself transported back to it, back to that moment and I'm dry retching, doubled over, holding onto the brick wall, hearing my heart hammering in my chest and it's all I can do to not fall on my knees.

When my panic subsides, as I remind myself that I'm not there, I'm not in that moment, I realise someone is behind me.

Watching me.

My heart slams into my chest once more and I turn quickly as their shadow looms over me. It's him. Nico.

He's followed me.

"What..?" I begin but I let my words fall. It's obvious why he's here. I glance around wondering for a second if he might just take his chances now that we're alone. If he's really the monster everyone says he is.

"I wouldn't let you wander these streets by yourself. It's not safe."

I scoff. Like he knows what's safe. Like he's even keeping me safe.

"I walk these streets every night." I say back.

His lips curl. "And who do you think makes sure you get home in one piece each time?"

My heart stops. Freezes. He's been following me home?

"What do you want?" I ask.

He steps nearer. Just one step but it's enough to make my heart race again. He smiles like he can hear it. Like he can tell the effect he has on my body.

"Don't play coy Eleri. You're not an idiot."

"And neither are you." I say back though I'm unsure why.

He lets out a low chuckle. "No I am not. I know what I want. And I always get it."

I half snarl. He's so fucking cocksure. So certain.

"Why do you want me?" I hiss. "I'm ugly. Ruined. Half blind." I say. It's true. My face is so marred, so destroyed from the acid they threw on me that I lost my right eye. There's nothing but melted flesh there now which is why I keep my hair down to hide it. To hide me.

"No man would want me. I'm a pariah in this city." I state.

He tilts his head at my words. "No darling." He says. "You are a queen. My queen. And I will make this entire city crawl on their knees before you."

I gasp as his words. He's mad. Insane. This monster, this man who wields more power than anyone should is saying such things to me.

"I will give you tonight…"

"And then what?" I say.

He smiles for a moment. "And then you are mine."

I push past him. I have to. I have to get away. As I run I have expect him to chase me down, to grab me, to make me stop.

When I get to the dingy bedsit that is my home I shut the door, sliding all the locks across. Not that they'd keep him out if he really wanted to get in. He could have his men smash the door in. Could shoot it off its hinges. No one would call the police. No one would dare. And even if they did it wouldn't make any difference because they answer to him too. They're on his pay.

I pace the room. There's barely enough space between the lumpy old couch and the bed. And it doesn't help that Sarpedon's enclosure takes up the entire space that was clearly designed for a dining table. I watch him for a moment, it's night, when he's most active, and with the heat lamp he's in his element. I bought him right after I got out of the hospital. For some reason it felt like a normal pet wouldn't cut it, and the fact he might live for the next fifty years was a definite appeal.

For the months that I spent locked up in this space, hiding, enduring surgery after surgery, this creature kept my company, kept me sane. He's the closest thing to a friend I've had because my old friends have long since deserted me.

After all who wants to be friends with a person as ugly as me? As broken as me? As disgusting as me?

I grab his dinner, I left it out to thaw so it would be nice and warm for him and as I put it down for him to see, he looks at me as if to say thanks. And then he pounces, wrapping his beautiful skin around it and for a moment I wince. I know the mouse is dead but still.

And then Nico's face flashes in my head. Suddenly I feel like that mouse, trapped, caught, ensnared. I can't escape him. I know that in my bones. Even if I packed my bags tonight and got the first bus out of here, he would know, he would find me, and he would drag me back.

But as I sink onto the couch I think of something even more disturbing, even more alarming; that maybe I don't want to escape him.

Maybe just maybe this man might not be my prison.

Maybe he might set me free.

Him

CHAPTER

Three

My knuckles are white. I'm clenching my fists, doing everything in my power not to beat the man in front of me to a pulp.

He's a lackey. A messenger. No one of importance really and in truth I'm giving him more credit than he's worth to be even in the same room as him right now.

I look over a Preston. His right eye is twitching, a sign that he's on edge.

Lackey boy says something. Words. Nothing of consequence and a few of my men smirk. He's amusing them because they don't have the sense to understand what's really going on. What this power play is.

I run the huge gold ring on my left little finger over my lips, tasting the metal, feeling it's coolness.

Lackey murmurs something and my eyes flit to him as I register them.

"What did you say?" I growl.

He hesitates for a millisecond and then he repeats it. The same taunt. The same hint of arrogance in his voice.

"They're willing to cut you a deal. To work with you."

"Work with me?" I say leaning forward. My arms rest on the table in front of me.

"On the proviso you defer to their authority." He adds.

My men shift. I can feel it, the way their body changes. This man is challenging me. Daring me. He comes into my kingdom, my domain and he dares to speak to me like that?

I shake my head slightly getting to my feet.

Preston murmurs my name. He's anxious. He knows we can fight them. He knows we can beat them but he's the cautious one out of the pair of us. The angel on my shoulder if you will.

I flex my hand stepping out from where I've been sat.

The lackey sizes me up as if he's a worthy opponent and as I inhale a deep breath of the air between us I feel it reverberate like an elastic band about to snap.

My fist slams into his face. My ring smashing his front teeth right out. He cries out in shock and pain but I barely hear it because I'm already striking him again.

He's on the floor within seconds. I raise my leg, kicking him hard and feeling the way his body moulds around my boot.

My men move around me. Their blood is up. They're as ready for this fight now as me.

My shoes slams into his jaw and I hear it crack with a pleasing crunch. I want it to be a message. I want this god forsaken piece of shit to crawl back on his hands to his pitiful masters.

And I want them to see it. For them to know that I did it. Not my men, not some errand boy, but me. That I'm not adverse to getting my hands dirty and when I get my hands on them that's exactly what I'll do. Dirty them with their blood.

When the man stops moving. When he's done fighting and he's simply laying there pathetic I step back and let my men drag his beaten body out of my bar.

"Was that necessary?" Preston says as we watch them.

"You rather I roll over like a dog?" I say.

"No. I know you better than that. But this, this starts a war."

"No this simply ends the ceasefire. We've been warring for months. It's been simmering long enough." I growl. I'm ready to fight. Ready to show this city exactly what it means when they try to rise up against their king, when they try to bite the hand that feeds.

Preston grunts in reply and then his eyes flicker across the room.

Eleri. She's here. Staring at me from across the bar. I knew she'd return but the look on her face is disarming.

She's not hiding herself for once. She stood facing me off as if she believes the words I said yesterday. As if I've fed her very soul. She crosses the room and I watch each minuscule move of her body. Each hint at what hides under the baggy clothing she persists in wearing.

One of the men steps forward to stop her and I raise my hand to tell him to back the fuck off.

And then I sit, like a king on my throne seeing my queen approaching and I know she's about to do my bidding.

She stops in front of me. Her eye running over my body in a way she's never dared before. It's incredible to see how she's grown in confidence in less than a day.

She sits on the stool the other side of the table and pulls something from her pocket.

"What is this?" I say.

"I have conditions."

"What conditions?"

"You have your wants and I have mine." She says so demurely, so matter of fact that my dick comes to life, hardens under the tightness of my pants. No woman talks to me like this. There's no game playing, no suggestions. She's so fucking perfect.

"Tell me." I say. My legs are still spread, if she chose to look she'd see the effect she's having on me and by god do I want her to. I want to grab that pouty little mouth of hers, shove her face hard into my crotch and let her feel exactly what she's doing.

"This man." She replies sliding the tatty photo towards me. "I want him dead."

I narrow my eyes glancing down at it. I don't know him. I don't recognise him. Not that I expected to but I feel a flash of something akin to jealousy at the thought that this could be an ex. Some past lover she's decided to get revenge on.

"Who is he?"

Her

CHAPTER

Four

I look at the image only briefly. I've stared at that photo for so long. It still surprises me that I had the nerve to take it. That after recognising him I had the balls to follow him. Figure out what decrepit little spaces of this city he occupies and then sneak back one day to take this. To record his face.

Of course I'd planned to get my revenge myself. I'd dreamt about it over and over. Of gutting the man. Of burying a knife so deep into his chest it came out the other side.

Only I'm not stupid enough to think I'd get close because he'd see me. They all would. Everyone sees me. Everyone stares.

They see my body first despite my best efforts to hide it and then they look at my face expecting to see a beauty and instead are met with horror.

"Who is he?"

I look up meeting his eyes. There's something there. Something in them. Is he annoyed? Angry even that I'm not just laying over for him. That I've asked for something in return as if his attention isn't enough for me.

"He's the one who destroyed my face." I say.

His eyebrows raise and he looks back down, picks up the photo and a smile that should send a shiver through me creeps across his lips.

"You want your dues darling?" He says.

"Yes."

He looks at me murmuring something under his breath and for a moment I take his face in. The hard lines. The thick brows. The scar that traces along his cheek that should make him ugly too only it doesn't. It enhances his appearance.

"Deal." He says pocketing the photo, getting to his feet and moving round towards me.

My fear lurches, just for a second as his hand grasps my arm pulling me to my feet.

The bar is filling up. Punters are starting to pour in and the other girls are watching whatever is happening between me and their boss with more than a little curiosity.

"Let's go." He says tugging me along.

"Where?"

He doesn't reply. It's almost as if he doesn't hear me. We're out the bar in seconds. His men are behind us. Ahead his blacked out SUV is humming and I can see a man stood by the open door waiting for his master.

"Where are we going?" I ask trying to stop. Trying to get some sort of control.

"You made a deal darling. We both have our ends to keep."

He nods to the chauffeur who makes a point of not looking at me and Nico tells me to get in. As I half clamber over the leather seats I wonder if I've made a mistake, a terrible, terrible misjudgement about this man.

I know he's dangerous. I know he runs the mob. He literally controls this entire city and now I've given myself to him like an idiot. I'm shaking before I can stop myself. Any attempt at pretence is gone.

He gets in beside me and watches me for a moment.

"Are you scared Eleri?" He asks.

I nod. There's no use in lying to him. He's not an idiot and the way he's staring at my throat suggests he can read my body well enough.

"Scared of me?"

I nod again.

He lets out a low laugh. It's disarming. My skin erupts into goosebumps as I hear it.

He takes my hand, places it on his crotch and I gasp as I feel how fucking hard he is right now.

"You have nothing to fear from me." He says. "I will treat you like my queen. Worship you as my only god." He states as he rocks his hips slightly.

I glance at the partition. It's obvious the driver can't hear us and part of me is relieved but the other part? The other part wants him to hear, wants everyone to hear, and that thought makes me think I must be mad too.

"Why me?" I say trying to keep my voice neutral despite the heat starting to flush in me. My fear is rapidly giving way to something akin to lust, reckless, stupid, illogical wants.

He lets out another laugh. "This is why." He says grinding harder. "You. You do this. You make me want in ways I've never wanted."

"But I haven't…"

"No Eleri. That's another why. You're a fucking saint. A wanton angel calling out for me alone, only you don't know you've been doing it."

I gulp unable to respond and he lets me fall silent, but he keeps his hand over mine. Keeps me gripping his cock. Part of me wants to pull mine free, to slip mine under the fabric and feel him but I don't dare and besides I have no idea where we're going right now. I don't know how long we'll be in this car and I don't want to start something I'm not ready for.

But as he undoes his belt I realise this is already happening. He's escalating. Making his move.

I bite my lip because in all honesty I'm probably as turned on right now as he is. I haven't been touched by anyone, been with anyone, even felt aroused in so long that this deep longing is building in me and I can't think of anything else except the fact that this man wants me. Me.

He doesn't tell me to do it. I do it because I want to. I move my other hand, slide it under his boxers and his dick springs free.

"Fuck." I murmur.

He's big. Ridiculously big. Maybe that's why he acts the way he does. He's all macho big dick energy and here's the reason.

I've not been with many men. I've had a handful of boyfriends before that night. Maybe the guys I was with before were just small. But as I stare at his cock I know that he's not normal. His dick is not normal.

"I can't fit that in." I say and he laughs.

"Yes you can. You'll take it all even if you gag on it." He says grabbing my head and pulling my face down to where I can see his precum is already glistening.

My lips touch the velvet softness of his head and he groans as if I've done something incredible.

I grab hold of him with my hands. The only way this will work is if I keep them at the base and try to limit how much his cock can get in. He's so girthy my fingers and thumbs don't even meet as they stretch around him.

I slide him inside and he groans again, shifting more in his seat so that he's more comfortable but it only increases the angle I'm at and I'm forced to get off from where I'm sat and kneel in the footwell at this man's feet.

He tilts his head staring at me and as I start to move him in and out of my mouth he pulls my hair back, gathers it into a rough ponytail at the nape of my neck and all of my face is revealed.

I wince. Wanting to hide. Needing to. But this man won't let me. His other hand is on top of my head, gripping me and forcing me to remain where I am.

"You look so good sucking my cock Eleri."

My mouth is so wide from how big his dick is I can't even respond but I feel the drool slipping out, sliding down my chin. I swirl my tongue over the tip of him, even his precum tastes like fucking heaven. This man must live off pineapple for him to taste so good.

I moan against him. I'm so turned on, even more so because of the danger of this. I should be scared, I should be resisting but I don't want to. I want Nico in this moment. I want his cock in my mouth. I want to be choking on him.

He grinds harder. He's thrusting with every move I make. I love the feel of his hand as his nails dig into my skin and for once I'm not even thinking about my face, about the fact that I'm bared open to him. I just want more. I need more.

"Fuck…" He lets out a long half growl and I shudder at the sound.

My hands are still round his cock. Both of them one on top of the other. I'm pumping at his base while my lips and tongue work the top of him but even like this he's still smacking into my tonsils.

He lets go of my hair, grabbing my hands with his one free and he forces them off. He wants me to take him all. I want to take him all. But there's a serious chance I will actually suffocate on him.

His grip tightens. He forces my head down further and further. My eye is streaming, tears are rolling my down cheek and my chin is covered in drool. I'm only grateful that I don't wear mascara because my face would be streaked with black.

He's thrusting more and more and his dick is merciless as it hits my throat and goes down it. I can't help it. I start gagging. I'm choking. Gasping for air but he doesn't relent. He keeps face fucking me and though I'm struggling I love it all the same. Because he clearly wants this. He wants me.

Nobody has ever used me like this. Needed me like this.

He's groaning more and more and I want to beg him to cum already. Beg him to pour his cum down my throat and fill me up.

As my breath starts to really catch, as I properly start to panic he cums. His warm salty delicious cum covers me, covers my tongue, coats my throat and I swallow it all, desperate for more.

He slides out of me just a little and I make sure to clean him. To massage his cock with my tongue and suck up every last bit of his juices.

"That's it angel. Suck me dry." He groans. And I do. I lick every inch of him. Honouring his cock with my tongue before finally letting him go.

His hand is on my face now. He's no longer gripping me with force but it feels almost loving. I can feel the warmth of his flesh, the roughness of it too and I wonder how he would feel, his skin against mine. He runs his thumb over the bottom of my scar and I look away.

He tuts annoyed and forces my face back. I'm still sat in the footwell. The car is gently rocking as it moves and I feel like I'm suddenly worshipping at this man's feet.

"Never be ashamed." He says.

"I'm ugly." I mutter it.

"Not to me you're not." He replies.

I stare back at him. My mouth is open, agape. I want to say something. To argue but I'm too dumbfounded to form any words. The car comes to a stop. The door opens and the chauffeur is stood not looking at either of us but waiting for Nico to get out.

I glance outside and I don't recognise where we are. Nico tucks his now flaccid cock back into his trousers and rearranges his clothes before stepping out. And then he holds his hand for me. As if I'm something of worth. As if I'm someone he's proud to be associated with.

I clamber out of the footwell. It's obvious to everyone what's gone on but the only person beside us is making a point of not looking.

Nico holds my hand and leads me into what looks like a god damn presidential palace.

Him

CHAPTER
Five

She's trembling. My fucking angel is a bag of nerves beside me and god do I want to rip her clothes off her right now and fuck her hard till her body jerks with pleasure and she sees there's nothing to be scared of.

The feel of my cock in her mouth was too much to resist. I didn't even mean to go that far but once her hand was on me and I could see the arousal in her face I knew I could push it.

And I knew she wanted me to.

Hell she fucking loved it. The way she gagged on my cock, the way she sucked me clean told me that.

I suppress a groan at the thought of it. If I hadn't cum so much I'd be hard again and all the men around us would see my throbbing erection.

But I can feel it, my arousal, my need for her. It's overriding my thinking. Overriding everything. This girl is so much more than I realised. So much more than I expected and I'm dying to have my taste too.

We climb the stairs. She doesn't ask where I'm taking her. She doesn't speak. We both know where we are. That this is my house. Her home now.

I like that she's quiet. I like that she doesn't ask pointless questions or see the need for small talk. This woman is perfection.

And as we walk along the corridor I can't help but smirk at the way her face darts around us, taking in the space, taking in her new surroundings.

I want her to look. I want her to see it all. The fine paintings. The luxurious furniture. This is all hers now. I will cover her in diamonds, dress her in silks. She deserves nothing but the best and from now on she will want for nothing.

Starting with my cock.

We enter my bedroom and her steps falter. I drop my hold on her hand and turn to look at her properly.

"I…" She begins but I know what's she's going to say. She thinks I'm going to fuck her. But I won't. Not yet. I'm not so impatient I want my dessert all in one go. Besides there's plenty of fun to be had in the unwrapping.

I put my finger over her lips to silence her. I could tell her with words. I could ease her fears but I won't. I like that she's on edge. I like that it feels like any minute she might crumble. After seeing her perfect mask of stoicism for so long it's good to finally meet the real Eleri. The girl I know is lurking beneath the surface. And by the time I'm done she won't be scared. She'll be a monster to be reckoned with.

A goddess no one will dare to cross.

I start unbuttoning her shirt. It's black. I think this girl only owns clothes in this one colour as if it would help her blend into the background. She swallows but she doesn't try to stop me.

As the shirt comes undone I see glimpses of her body beneath and my mouth waters. Fuck me this girl has curves. Real curves. She's built exactly as I imagined and some. I yank the shirt off desperate to see her now.

Her breath hits me as she starts to take in short bursts almost as if she's hyperventilating.

"I'm going to make you feel good." I say and she nods but I can see in her face the fear is still there.

I push her back, force her to move back and she stumbles before falling onto my bed. Her hair falls splayed. Her legs are open almost teasingly and I'm half tempted to rip her jeans off now that I can.

I crawl over her. My body on top of hers and she lets out the tiniest almost imperceptible whimper and at the sound my dick comes back to life. My blood starts pouring into it and it takes all my focus to keep myself calm.

Because this is about taking my time. Now that I have her, now that she's within my grasp I need to tease the wanton part of her out, nurture the goddess inside her and build her up as the fierce woman I know she is.

I let my hand caress her starting with the swell of her waist and then I move up her stomach to where her breasts hang like forbidden fruit waiting for me to devour them.

They're so big they can fill both my hands with just one perfect peak. I bury my face between her cleavage and her body responds. She arches her back. Her legs widen more and she gasps.

My perfect fucking queen gasps.

I look up at her. From this angle you can see exactly how her face should have been. How beautiful she was before.

I grab at the cup encasing her right tit and I yank it down. Her nipple is big. Incredibly so. No dainty little circles here. Just an unashamed coronet of perfection. I suck it in, needing her in my mouth. She moans as I do it and fuck does it make me suck harder. My hand massages her, my tongue teases her. Her nipple gets harder and harder and in that moment I don't think. I just act. I bite her. I bite hard and she jerks, crying out in shock.

But her body is already melting, giving into me because while my main focus has been on her incredible breasts my other hand has been undoing her jeans.

I slide in between her panties and they're soaked. Drenched. It can't be just from this moment. She must have been dripping out while my cock was buried down her throat.

"Is this all for me?" I say twirling my fingers in amongst the sopping fabric and she turns so red I laugh. "Don't be embarrassed darling. I like that you're this wet because you should be."

She meets my gaze but she doesn't reply. I can see she's torn between her arousal and some voice in her head that's still screaming danger.

"You got to taste me. Now it's my turn." I say sliding my fingers between her folds, feeling her sticky wet arousal as she spreads herself wider, inviting me to do what I want.

Her fear gone now, her need for me completely overriding it.

She feels so smooth. I expected hair, I expected at least a strip of it but the fact that there's nothing but her bare skin makes me curious. I wonder what she'd look like, her cunt wide open and exposed for me. As my fingers move we hear the slick sounds of it and it spurs me on. I want to make her so wet all we can hear is her cunt dripping like a tap.

I suck her nipple back into my mouth and plunge my fingers inside her. She groans, writhing, encouraging me more like I need any encouragement.

I start working her away. Curling, pushing against her G spot to get her closer to where I want her. She moans more. Delicious, loud moans that make me half lose my focus.

My dick is throbbing so hard in my pants. All I can think of is burying it in her but she's not ready. Even now, even while she's coming apart at my touch she's not ready for all of me. I yank the bra down properly, finally free her breasts and they flop so beautifully in front of my face. I grab the breast I've been ignoring and the nipple hardens at my touch. Her body is so obedient to me. So perfectly trained already.

I stare at her face, watching her move, watching her enjoy every second of what I'm doing to her.

Fuck she is perfect. My perfect fucking queen.

I grin, lowering my mouth to her breast once more and then a knock at the door makes me stop.

Makes us both stop.

I narrow my eyes. My fingers are still deep in her cunt and I don't want to take them out and from the look on her face she doesn't want me to either.

"What?" I growl.

"It's Emerson." Preston says through the wood. But of course it fucking is.

I shake my head looking at my angel. I can see in her eye she wants me to ignore it. To pretend it's just us. But this kingdom won't run itself.

And I have traitors in my midst. Traitors that need to be eliminated if only to keep my wanton queen here safe.

"Wait here. I'll be back." I say pulling my fingers out and her body physically deflates.

"I…" She starts and then nods, looking around as if she's only just realised she's in my bedroom. "What do I do while you're gone?" She asks.

My eyebrows raise for a second. She sounds unsure. She sounds unconfident. The high walls this girl has built seem to have turned to dust but I don't believe it's just from me touching her. I'm not a romantic. Shit like that doesn't happen.

"Have a shower. There's fresh clothes for you. Make yourself at home." I say standing up, trying to tuck my dick under my belt to hide my erection.

"Home." She says quietly. Like she's never had one. Like she doesn't know the meaning of the word and that again I file away for later. Something to explore. Something more to understand about her.

"This is your home now." I state and she looks confused.

I go to leave. The sooner I've dealt with this shit-show the sooner I can turn my attention back to Eleri.

"And don't leave this room." I add before shutting the door.

CHAPTER

Six

The door clicks and for a moment I think he might have locked me in. I guess I'd be more relieved if he had because then I wouldn't have a choice but to obey him.

I lay back on the bed. His bed. I can smell him. Something musky, rich wood undertones, and vanilla too. As I breathe it in it fills my nostrils and my heart hammers harder in my chest.

I'm fucking crazy I realise. I'm here in a mob king's house. In his bed. Half-naked or as good as and I've let him already take too much from me. I should have resisted. Should have played hard to get. That's what all the girls at the bar would have done. That's all they ever went on about. How men respected girls that didn't lay it all out. How you had to wait to at least date three before you get down to any action.

And yet here I am, not even date one with my pussy still aching from where his fingers where in me and haven't finished their mission.

I groan in annoyance. In confusion. In frustration too.

My tits are still out. My bra is folded over uncomfortably and I roll over unhooking it and tossing the damn thing. They always make bras so ugly for women of my size. If I was a b cup, or even a c, I'd be able to buy something pretty, delicate, sexy. But when you're an e cup all sexiness goes out the window.

And in truth. I've not exactly been looking for sexy underwear. It wasn't high on my list. But then letting my boss finger fuck me wasn't high up there either and look where I am now.

I glance around, at Nico's bedroom. It's so ornate it feels unreal. That this man sleeps here. That this is really his space. The bed is so big it must be a custom. The sheets are black silk. The mattress underneath me is holding my body in a way no other mattress has ever done and part of me wants to climb under the duvet and bury myself further into it.

I get up deciding to have a shower, more because when Nico comes back I have no doubts he's going to want to continue what he started and I at least want to be cleaner. More prepared.

The bathroom is just as ridiculous as the bedroom. A huge sunken bath is at one end. There's a double sink vanity made from what looks like marble. And tucked around a wall is a walk-in shower that has the biggest rain-shower head I've ever seen.

I slip my jeans off, and leave them in a pile with my panties tucked up inside; some futile attempt at decency though all mine appears to have left me the minute I got in that damn car. There's a neatly stacked row of towels under the vanity and a silk bath robe hanging from a gold hook.

On the side there's a hair brush and I take my time working out the knots from where Nico has tangled it all up.

And then I stare at myself in the full length mirror. Stare at my body. I only have one mirror in my place. A tiny cracked thing above the rickety sink and I only adjust it to cover the scar across my face, to try to blur it more.

But now I'm seeing me for the first time in two years.

I tilt my head, taking in how fat my thighs look, how round my hips are. My breasts are slightly saggy but with the size they are I'm not surprised. I don't look beautiful but I'm not ugly either. The only problem is my body doesn't conform to the size zero ideal that the world screams to demand of women.

I'm not a perfectly sculpted mass of muscle and lithe limbs. I'm fleshy. Curvy. Voluptuous.

Old me used to like my body. Used to like the way I stood out but ever since my attack I've kept myself hidden. Concealed. It's not that I'm ashamed of how I look, it's that my body caused this, caused those men to do what they did and now my face bears the repercussions.

I sigh walking into the shower and turn it on. The water pours down and the pressure makes it feel like I'm in a monsoon. It's incredible. I let out a laugh, turning up the heat, revelling in the feel of it against my skin.

I feel alive. I feel awake.

And then I think of Nico. Of what his hands did to me. How his fingers felt inside me.

He wasn't holding back. He didn't seem to care what my face is like, hell he said as much. But the way he reacted, the way he was touching me, grabbing me, needing me. Am I being naïve to think it was real? Am I getting lost in some fantasy world to think that this might be what my life is from now on? By this man's side? His woman?

I shake my head at the absurdity. Nico could have any woman he wanted. Any woman at all. So why would he chose me? And yet he had. He did. I was in his bed, with his fingers as far in my pussy as he could shove them.

I groan again. Between my thighs is an ache I can't get rid of. I haven't felt turned on, aroused, felt anything in truth in two years. Sex isn't a thing for me. It doesn't do anything. I just don't have those feelings. Not anymore.

And yet less than an hour ago I was so turned on I would have willingly choked to death on Nico's cock and I would have thanked him for it.

I don't even know who I am right now. Who I've become. In the space of twenty four hours my life has gone from one of existing, to something else entirely.

As my pussy throbs I move my hand to touch myself. Hell, if Nico can make me actually feel something then maybe I can finish this. Maybe I can actually cum again.

I'm still wet and I know it's not from the water coming over head. The consistency is wrong. The way it sticks to my lips is wrong too. I move my legs wider apart, leaning back against the tiles. I'm aroused. I'm needy. I want to feel this. I want to cum.

I rock my hips, my fingers aren't even inside me yet because I'm still lost imagining how full I felt with Nico's in me. And then as I think again of how he plunged them into me the first time I do it, I penetrate myself.

Fuck it feels so good. I throw my head back. I let out a moan and wonder if anyone can hear me.

My fingers aren't as long as Nico's but I remember how I used to touch myself. How I used to make myself cum. I start pumping away. Working up the pressure. My breasts are heaving as my heartrate steadily increases and I imagine Nico is here, watching me because for some reason that notion turns me on. A lot.

I run my other hand up my body, pinching, squeezing my nipple, hurting the one he bit because I want to feel the pain again. I want his teeth on me. I want his mouth claiming me.

My legs start shaking and I realise I'm there, I'm about to cum. I blink back the tears but they're already falling and, as my euphoria takes over, I start screaming a sound of pleasure as well as relief. Joy as well as fear.

My body jerks, my fingers move haphazardly because I'm not ready to let my orgasm go. I can feel my cum dripping down my legs, mixing with the shower water.

He did this. He fixed me.

The words linger in my head more than they should. More than is sane.

And I lie back against the tiles panting, thinking of when Nico will come back, how hard it will be to resist him now and if I even want to.

Him

CHAPTER

Seven

I'm sat across from Preston. He can tell from my face how pissed I am. The fact that he pulled me from her though tells me something. Blaine walks in and sits down, sliding a file across the table.

"The fuck is this?" I growl.

"Take a look." Blaine says. "It's the proof we've been looking for."

I narrow my eyes, half snatching at the paper and open it. There's dozens of photos. Dozens of scraps of paper too. All evidence of what's really been going on behind my back.

"Where did you get this?" I ask.

"I had to get resourceful." He smirks. Of course he did. Blaine is nothing if not resourceful. That's why I hired him. Why he's my head of security.

ELLIE SANDERS

Preston watches me curiously and I slide the documents to him.

He takes his time examining each piece.

"We need to hold fire. I don't want the Dalconti's knowing we have this just yet." I say.

Blaine nods but Preston looks dubious. "It's a risk. You've already beaten up one of the Le Cruso guys. You think they'll just wait?"

I shrug. "If they make any moves we will counter them but I want to bring them down my way. I want to annihilate them."

Preston nods and Blaine grins, his signature, golden toothed grin.

"We should double security." Blaine says.

"Yes." I reply.

"What about the girl?" Preston says.

"What girl?" Blaine asks looking between us.

"Nico took one of the girls from the bar." Preston says so flippantly I feel my blood surge.

"She's none of your concern." I growl.

"Mighty convenient you decide to bring someone back with all this going on…" Blaine says as if Eleri could be a spy.

"That's a fair point." Preston says.

"Eleri has nothing to do with this."

"You're sure?" Preston says.

"Certain." I say.

Preston grunts in reply like he's not convinced but I don't give a shit. I know she's got nothing to do with this because I picked her. She didn't thrust herself into my life, at least not the way they're implying. I've watched her every move for the last two years. If she was involved I'd know about it.

"Blaine see to the security. Preston, I want you out tonight." I say.

"You're staying in?" Preston says surprised, as if he doesn't know exactly why I would be.

I don't reply. I just wait for them both to leave and then I sit, thinking for a moment about what Blaine found. About the fact that my own family is working against me. My own brother is instigating this. Again.

I let out a sigh and my mind wanders to the beguiling creature I left in my room. I've left her for too long but I'm curious as to what she's been up to. How she might act while she thinks she's alone. Will she go through my things? Will she simply curl up in my bed and wait patiently for me?

I pull my phone and flick to the app that connects to the cameras I had installed. Even Blaine doesn't know about these ones.

She's there, drying herself. I can see her body reflected in a blur on the mirror. Apparently she followed my instructions to the letter about what to do in my absence.

Switching to a different camera I rewind the feed back and watch as my angel steps fully naked into my shower. Fuck she's more magnificent than I imagined. Her ass is so fat I want to bury my face in it and suffocate between her cheeks. The water is pouring over her body and as I watch she begins to wash herself.

I smirk, wondering if she knows I've put these cameras up but of course she doesn't. She doesn't have a fucking clue.

My jezebel. My wanton queen, revealed now for me to leer at and for her to be completely unaware.

And then she does something unexpected. She starts touching herself. Pleasuring herself.

I shift in my chair, clear my throat, sit up and lean over the screen, half wishing I could zoom in on the action but I'm enthralled at how her body is writhing, moving as she brings herself closer and closer to climax.

Did I leave her so desperate, so sexually frustrated that she had to grant her own form of release? My lips curl at the thought. That her cunt was so hungry after my fingers left that she needed to feed it with her own hand.

She writhes, her mouth opens and I know she is moaning though the feed is silent. As I watch her she cums hard, her body jerking as if this release is giving more than just simple pleasure. I swear there are tears down her face but I must be imagining it unless she's one of those people who cries when she cums? I'm not going to lie the thought intrigues me and I want to make her cum to see if she cries as my fingers grant her a mercy only I can bestow from now on.

My cock is throbbing, leaking precum from watching this and as I realise, I'm on my feet I move to the door. I want to see her cum for me now. I want to hear her moans as I tear her apart with my fingers.

"Nico." The door opens and Preston is there, looking alarmed.

My eyes snap to him. "What now?" I growl.

"Shit's hit the fan." He says showing me his phone and the news alert that's flashing across it.

"What the fuck?" I snap. "How are we hearing this from the press?"

Preston shakes his head holding the door for me to walk out. I don't even try to hide my erection. I don't give a fuck if they can see.

"We've got cars ready."

I grunt. Fat lot of good that will do now. They've attacked one of our convoys. Stolen our merchandise. Does he really think simply showing up and saying a few words will fix this?

Blaine is there, waiting. I can see from his face he's just as pissed as me.

We walk out of the house. Blaine and Preston just behind me and as I get in the back of my car I glance up thinking I might see her. Only I know I won't. My room is at the back of the house and she's no doubt already wondering what's keeping me so long.

I shake my head. My dick is still throbbing. Aching. I'm half tempted to ignore this entire situation and storm back inside but I know my own pleasure will have to wait.

Eleri will have to wait.

If she's truly to be the queen I want her to be then this is a good lesson in learning that I will not always be able to put her needs first. And better we start off this way, with no false promises. No pretence. Just her sleeping alone, in my bed, while my cock leaks out with a want only she will satisfy.

CHAPTER

Eight

He doesn't come back.

I sit, I wait for what feels like hours. In my stupidity I thought he'd return before it got late but the whole night passes and there's nothing. It's not that I'm upset that he left me, it's not that it feels like he's abandoned me though in a way he has, I'm more concerned for where he is. What would keep him away when he so obviously wanted to stay?

While he was gone I went through the wardrobes. Not to be nosy but simply because I needed to wear something.

One side was full of his clothes, his suits, his shirts, everything tailored to fit his body. His shoes were polished, lined up neatly beneath like some sort of statement I can't fathom.

But the other side, is full of dresses, tops, skirts, you name it. It's all in my size. All with tags still on. Beneath are dozens of high heels. And in the drawers are enough pieces of lingerie to fill a Victoria Secrets catalogue. I blush as I pull some of the panties out. Their lacy, sheer, sexy as hell.

And again, all of it is in my size.

How long has this man had this planned? Because that's what it feels like. A plan. A set up. My heart is thumping because this can't be a coincidence. There's no way this is all some spontaneous, knee jerk reaction. He's up to something. I just can't get my head around what.

My queen. That's what he called me.

Those were the exact words he used.

But I'm not his queen. I can't be. And yet all of this behaviour, everything he has done since he confronted me two days ago says what his intentions are.

I didn't want to sleep in his bed. It felt weird to be in his space without him. Too intimate. Though in truth I think it would feel even stranger to be here with him. I barely know the man. Until two days ago I haven't said one word to him.

And yet as soon as I got under the covers, as soon as the smell of him overwhelmed me, I drifted off into the deepest, heaviest slumber I've had in a long time.

So now I'm lying, wearing nothing but a satin slip that was laid out pointedly for me to see, in his bed. As if any of this was normal.

I roll over, trying to shut the stupid thoughts in my head up.

"Morning darling." He says softly, his hand stroking my cheek as I gasp.

I didn't even hear him come in. I didn't even realise he was here. The man is a ghost. A god damn demon.

He chuckles at my shock. "Have I scared you again?" He says.

"No. You just made me jump." I say back.

His lips curl.

"Why didn't you come back? What happened?" I ask before I can stop myself.

"Just some business that needed taking care of." He replies. He looks tired. He looks like he hasn't slept.

Perhaps he can see the concern in my face because he moves to lay down beside me with his arms pulling my body into his.

I shut my eye, welcoming his embrace, welcoming his touch too despite the absurdity of this situation, despite the fact I barely know this man.

He buries his face in my hair, sniffing it.

"You had a shower." He murmurs.

I nod. "You told me too."

"Do you like following my orders?" He says.

"There wasn't anything else to do with you gone." I state. It's not meant to sound like a criticism and I hope he doesn't take it as one. He's a busy man. He's got a lot more important things going on than me and I don't want him to think I'm the sort of high drama girl that demands attention twenty four hours a day.

"No?" He says almost teasingly, moving his hand, pulling his phone from his pocket.

"No." I reply biting my lip. I feel like we're both flirting so badly now but I'm also infinitely aware of the fact I'm not really wearing very much at all.

He moves his screen so that I can see and pushes a play button. I frown realising with horror what he's showing me. It's me. It *was* me. In the god damn shower. He put camera's up. He...

I gulp seeing as I'm there, naked, masturbating for this man to watch.

"You..." I say but I shake my head before I can get any words out.

"Do you know how hard it was to see this, to watch you cum and not just race in here and fuck you?"

I gulp. I can hear his arousal. I can see it too. His pupils are dilated. He looks like a feral beast right now. A wolf about to devour me.

"I didn't know you had cameras." It's all I can say. It's a stupid thing to say and he laughs.

"I didn't expect them to be so useful." He murmurs.

His hand is brushing my hair back, my skin tingles as his fingertips scrape against me.

"I've not..." I begin and then I force the words out. "I've not cum in over two years."

He pauses. His eyes meet mine. But he doesn't say anything, as if he gets that this moment, this fraction of time is what I need for me.

"I couldn't. I didn't want to. I've not even felt remotely aroused." I state.

"Not once?" He says and I shake my head.

"Why not?" He asks.

I look away unable to hold his gaze. It's not like I'm going to cry, it just feels weird, to be having this conversation with anyone, but especially to be having it with Nico Morelli. "After what happened I didn't want to feel it. I didn't want anyone to see my like that, to want me like that."

"You are not responsible for what happened." He says, stroking my face, caressing the outline of my scar as if he understands where it came from, as if he knows my past.

I wince as the feel of his fingers turn to numbness, turn to nothing with where all my sense of touch has gone.

"Why did you put those cameras up?" I ask. It's not like I really care but it's a good way to change the topic. To redirect it. To get the focus off a part of my life I'd rather not discuss.

"I like watching you. And I like the way you are when you think no one is there. When you think no one is observing you. You come out of your shell. You become yourself."

"Huh." I reply. He's a voyeur. I hadn't pegged him as that despite all the times I've felt his eyes on me when I've been working. "So…" I put my hand on his chest. "Did it turn you on to see me like that?"

He grins. Like he likes the fact I'm not being coy. And in truth I'm surprised by it too. I guess my old self is closer to the surface than I realised.

"It would turn me on more to make you cum." He says pulling the covers off from me and taking in the satin slip. "You're wearing it."

"I thought it would be rude not to." I say.

He starts yanking it up my thighs in quick bursts. "Very rude." He agrees as he exposes my entire lower half to him.

I move my legs wider. Just a little.

"You are keen." He says.

"I've not cum in over two years. You did that. You gave me that."

He nods moving so that his body is on me and his face is parallel to my pussy. "So is this my reward?"

"Do you want it to be?" I say. Fuck I'm so turned on right now I think I'm actually shaking. He's staring at me like he's never seen a naked woman before. Like what lies between my thighs is his only path to salvation.

"My reward will be you cuming all over my tongue while you scream my name." He states.

I nod almost mindlessly. He could say anything right now and I'd agree because I'm so desperate for him. Desperate to feel him. Desperate to have him touch me.

His tongue does a long slow swipe along me and I groan.

"Spread your legs more. I want to feast on this fat cunt of yours." He says.

And I do it. I spread my legs wide. As wide as they'll go.

His tongue laps at me. In great slurping motions. I rock my hips, enjoying every second of his undivided attention now that I have it. His fingers begin to probe me and I moan out as they slowly slide inside and my body welcomes them.

"Your cunt is so inviting." He groans as he spreads his fingers wider, opening me up for him slip tongue inside, licking me out.

"Oh god." I cry out.

"There are no gods here Eleri. Just you and me." He murmurs. His hot breath caresses my flesh almost as deliciously as his fingers are.

He starts twisting them, pumping away. He's got three fingers in me. It feels so tight. And I wonder if he's prepping me ready for his cock. His lips move to my clit. He begins sucking, rolling it over his tongue, and I wilt. Jesus I wilt. I mewl. I become some hot mess that can barely contain herself.

My legs kick out, my body starts gyrating as if I want to face fuck him and he sits back watching me as his fingers move to take over this new delicious torture.

"Oh fuck. Oh god." I'm shouting I realise. I've never shouted, not like this.

"That's it my queen." He says. "Come apart for me."

And I do. I don't even realise how I'm moving but as his fingers massage my clit I lose myself in waves of undulating pleasure. I throw my head back, it feels like my skull is trying to escape my body but I love every minute of it. I scream. I scream so loud and it's his name on my lips. Even if he hadn't told me to say it. Even if he hadn't said he wanted to hear it, I'd be calling for him. Crying for him. Cuming for him.

As I start to come down he stays where he is, watching, staring at my pussy and up at where the slip has shifted and my left breast is making an obvious bid for freedom.

I must look a mess. I must look an absolute state but from the way he's admiring me you wouldn't think it.

I try to move the slip, to at least make myself decent but he grabs at the fabric preventing me and he gives me a firm, don't argue with me look. So I lay there, with my tit exposed and my pussy open and used, right in front of his face as if I'm not embarrassed. As if I'm not self-conscious.

"Have you ever squirted?" He asks.

I look down at him shaking my head. "No. My body doesn't do that."

He laughs. "Oh it will." He replies. "I just need to find the right buttons to press."

I frown. He's so cocksure. So certain of everything. In a way I like it. I like his confidence and I like the way he sounds like he has plans for me.

He moves to lie beside me and I roll over to face him. He's still wearing his shirt and trousers from yesterday.

Slowly I unbutton it revealing the luscious god like physique below. To say this man has muscles is an understatement. My fingertips graze the small patch of hair on his chest. Normally it would turn me off but on him it only emphasises his masculinity.

"Like what you see?" He says as my mouth practically salivates as the sight of him watching me as I appraise him.

I nod.

He runs a finger down between my breasts, right into the deepest bit of my cleavage.

"Just like I like what I see." He says.

I blink in response but my hands are already moving to undo his belt. He tilts his head, taking over before yanking his trousers and boxers off in one go.

My eyebrows raise at the sight of him. At the sight of his fucking huge dick. He's hard. But I knew that already. He looks even more impressive from this angle. But he also looks dangerous. I think this man could actually hurt me if he wanted to. His dick could literally spear me.

He sees where I'm looking but he doesn't make any moves, any comments either. I reach out to touch him. To see if it's even real and he stops me.

"Not yet." He says.

"Why?"

"I need to sleep and you are not ready." He states.

"You don't know that." I say.

He smirks as if he knows me better than I know myself.

"I'm not going to rush this. I want us to both enjoy the unwrapping." He says as if he wasn't the one making me choke on his cock yesterday. "Sleep." He says pulling my body around so that he is spooning me.

I shut my eye. It's hard to try to. It's hard to focus on anything but the raging erection poking into my back. Taunting me almost. Begging for me to sit on it.

Him

CHAPTER
Nine

I can feel her squirming against me. I can feel my dick as it throbs against her. I'm leaking precum onto her skin. I'm half tempted to roll her back over and just fuck her despite my words. Despite my declarations.

I know she's not tired. That unlike me she probably got a decent enough amount of sleep last night. I know I'm being selfish in making her sleep right now but I don't care. I'm too tried to care. After everything that's happened in the last eight or so hours I just need at least a few hours to recuperate.

I can smell her scent. I can taste her on my tongue still. When I close my eyes I see her splayed out before me. Her divine body quivering with each touch I make. I lick my lips and I taste her there too. My face is covered in her. I don't want to wash. I don't want the smell of her gone. I'd walk around for the rest of my days, smothered in her juices, marked for everyone to know.

My hands move of their own accord. I'm caressing her skin, drawing lazy circles across her bare shoulder. I pull her hair aside and kiss her neck, seeing the hint of something behind her ear. As I tilt her head to get a better look I realise what it is. A tattoo. A snake. A viper. It's tiny, hidden enough that that you'd have to know it was there or she'd have to have her hair all pulled up for you to notice. It's so perfect. So ridiculously Eleri I can't help but smile.

"I've had it for years." She murmurs.

"What made you get it?" I ask running my finger over it. It's beautiful, delicate, a true piece of art, just like the woman in my arms.

"I like snakes. They're misunderstood creatures. They normally avoid people and only attack when provoked."

"Sounds a lot like you." I murmur and she shakes her head but I know it's true. This woman is deadly, she just needs to realise it too.

She gasps for a moment and then looks at me.

"What?" I ask.

"Sarpedon." She says. "I left him…" She turns to face me properly. "If you want me to stay here then I need to bring him."

"Sarpedon is your pet?" I say as if I don't already know it. As if I'm not aware of the frozen mice and god knows what else she orders to feed the thing.

"Yes." She says almost defiantly as if she expects me to challenge her, as if she expects me to want her to give up this part of herself for me.

"I've already sorted it." I state. "Some of my men have brought him over. I had a new enclosure built for him. It's bigger than what he's used to but I doubt he'll be disappointed."

She shakes her head as a grin creeps across her face. "Thank you."

"Don't thank me. I had a vested interest in doing so."

"Because you want me not to fight you?" She says as if she's even made an attempt.

"No Eleri, that's not it at all." I reply. "I want you to be happy. This is your home and that snake is part of your life. I'm not so cruel as to demand you leave everything behind for me."

She sighs looking almost relieved by my words and curls back into my arms.

"You might like him." She says.

I smirk. I'm not a pet person. Dogs have a use. Cats are arseholes but I like them for it. Snakes? Snakes are a whole different thing entirely, but this creature is important to her, to my woman, so I guess it's important to me too now.

I start circling her skin again, soothing her almost, though in truth her presence is soothing me. For a moment I think of the men who maimed her, who dared to touch her and my anger flares.

I gave the photo over to Blaine. He doesn't know who the man is and why I want him but he's already got some guys on it. And when he's found I'm going to present him to Eleri as a gift. I'm going to carve him up, cut him to pieces and I hope she has the tenacity to watch as I do it.

I want her to watch.

I want her to see how he suffers.

He scarred her flesh, he took half her sight, but her wounds will be nothing compared to the agony I will make him suffer.

I pause listening to her breathing. She's not asleep. She's not even trying but she seems content to lie here and pretend and I think in this moment I like her even more for it.

It's been a rough twelve hours since I took her. Since I agreed to her deal and made her mine. It's not how I planned this. In my head I would have wooed her more. Shown her exactly what it means to be my queen, what it means to belong to me.

She would know by now what my intentions were and this strange ambiguity wouldn't exist.

When I've rested I will make sure she is happy here. That she learns her way around, that my staff know her and treat her with respect. That she has everything she needs.

But right now I need my sleep. I need to get my own energy back.

And then I can deal with the larger problem, the real problem, the reason certain individuals think they even stand a chance of usurping me; my brother.

CHAPTER

Ten

I slip from the bed. As much as I enjoy being in his arms I can't lay here any longer or I think I'll go insane. It's been hours since he fell asleep. Hours that I've lain here with my head spinning over what this is, what this could be.

I'm bored. Bored of pretending to sleep. And I'm starving too.

I look down at him, at Nico, and he looks so deeply asleep I wonder if he would even notice a bomb going off.

But as I let out a low sigh his face clearly registers the noise and I realise I need to get out of this room. I need to leave him to it or I'll wake him up and I don't want to do that.

He clearly needs his sleep. He needs to rest.

I grab the same silk robe from the bathroom I used yesterday and wrap it around myself.

As quietly as I can I tiptoe out into the hallway beyond and shut the door. There must be a kitchen here. Even if all they have is some measly toast and coffee I'd settle for that. Hell, I'd settle for anything right now because with all the drama of yesterday I didn't have any dinner and I'm practically ravenous.

I make my way through this house. His home. There are so many doors. So many rooms it feels ridiculous. I don't want to look like I'm snooping but I open each one looking about, shutting them just as quickly when I realise they're not the room I'm after.

I half creep down the stairs. My bare feet pitter patter on the wood as I walk. If the kitchen is going to be anywhere I'd reason it was on this level.

I haven't seen anyone. There's no way it's just me and Nico in his house right now but the thought that we're not alone makes me uncomfortable. I don't trust people. It's not in my nature. And especially not after everything that's happened.

I'm even suspicious of Nico. Deep down, despite everything he's done so far I don't believe he won't hurt me in the end.

Because that's what everyone does.

"Who are you?" Someone says behind me and I cry out jumping as I turn.

"I…" My voice catches in my throat. I step back away from the angry looking man towering over me.

"I said who the fuck are you?" He growls pulling a gun from the holster at his waist before slamming me back into the wall behind me and shoving the barrel right under my jaw.

"Calm down Blaine. It's just the girl." Preston says coming up behind him.

"This is her?" He replies looking me up and down like a piece of gone off meat.

I narrow my eye at him.

"What the fuck happened to you?" He says staring at my face. He's probably one of the few men who've looked at me without quickly looking away.

"That's enough." Preston murmurs. He doesn't know my story but he knows enough from the bar to at least be respectful to a point.

"Her face is fucked." Blaine says. "Her skin is all..."

"What the hell is this?" Nico growls and I feel my stomach drop at the sound of his voice. He's awake.

"Your girl here went for a wander and Blaine found her." Preston states as Blaine steps back from me.

Nico narrows his eyes grabbing my arm, yanking me to him and I yelp at the force of it.

"I thought I told you not to leave my room." He says.

"I was hungry." I reply. "And I didn't want to wake you."

He stares at me for a moment as if trying to detect a lie and then he sighs like he's only just realising I haven't eaten a thing since he brought me here.

"I was just trying to find the kitchen." I say dropping my head, letting my hair fall to cover my face.

Blaine snorts as though I'm telling some outlandish joke.

Nico looks at him, taking in the gun still in his hand. "Put that away." He says quietly.

Blaine nods doing as he's told and I wonder who the hell he is. What his relation to Nico is.

"Let's go." Nico says pulling me along and away from them both.

I don't speak. I know I've pissed him off but it wasn't my intention.

We make it to the kitchen which is another ridiculously oversized room with two massive islands in the middle, both with waterfall sides of glistening marble.

One wall is just glass bi-folds as if the whole side can be opened up and I can see a balcony beyond. I'm staring at the view beyond before I realise Nico is staring at me.

I turn to face him and he's standing, arms crossed, face like thunder. Shit.

"I'm sorry…" I begin.

"I told you to stay in my room."

"I know but I couldn't sleep anymore and I knew you needed to."

He lets out a low breath.

"I didn't want to wake you by tossing and turning and besides I thought it might be nice to cook you something for when you woke up."

His eyebrows raise. "You can cook?"

I smile. It feels like one of us needs to defuse the situation and I'm okay for it to be me. I mean I did cause this didn't I?

"Yeah." I say moving up to him.

He's still watching me with something in his eyes.

"When I tell you to do something I need to know you'll listen." He says grabbing my upper arms and gripping them so tightly. "And that you'll obey."

"I will." I say quickly. Maybe too quickly. I don't know how to appease him. I'm not experienced enough with charming men and I sure as hell don't know how to handle a man like Nico. Not really.

The air feels charged. It feels like he's not convinced and I don't know why I do it but I do. I lift my head, brush my lips against his and as our skin touches it's like he goes wild.

He grabs me, pushing me back against the counter, his tongue is deep in my mouth. His lips are moving so roughly I think my lips will bruise. And by god do I want them to.

80

I moan out in shock, in pain, but in need too. Suddenly I need this man. I need him to devour me. To overwhelm me. To prove that this isn't just a moments fancy.

One of his hands grasp my hair, he's yanking on it so hard. I grab his back wanting him to know that I want him just as much. Giving every signal I can that I need him to keep going.

I feel my robe coming undone and his spare hand grabs my breast, rubs it, massages it and I moan again. Fuck this man seems to know how to manipulate my body in ways I've never felt before.

"Eleri." He groans my name into my mouth and I writhe against him. I love the way I sound on his lips. I love the way he pronounces my name as if I'm someone of worth.

My hands run down his naked chest. He's wearing a pair of joggers that he probably threw on just to come and find me and I take full advantage of there being only the thinnest fabric between my pussy and his cock.

He groans as I start rubbing against him. Grinding.

He yanks my hair back, pulling my neck at an impossible angle so that I have to arch my back to its full extent and my tits are pushed right forward. He stares at them, hungers for them then meets my eye.

"Fuck me." I say it before I can stop myself.

"Not yet." He says.

"I want you inside me."

"All in good time my love." He says and I frown. Why is he waiting? Why is he so hesitant? I'm obviously willing so what's the issue?

His fingers slide up my thigh and I bite my lip. Maybe he won't fill me with his cock but his fingers are a pretty good substitute. I shift my legs slightly and he smirks seeing the motion.

"Does your needy cunt need filling that much?" He says.

"Yes." I gasp not caring how desperate I sound.

He laughs in amusement and I grin too.

"Use me Nico." I say.

"I'm not going to do that." He says as his fingers slide into me so slowly. "I'm going to honour you. Worship you. Treat you like the goddess you are."

He curls his fingers and I let out a moan as hot wet arousal leaks out from me.

"Sorry to break this up." Preston says loudly from across the room and Nico snarls moving enough to block the view.

"What do you want?" Nico asks. His fingers are still in me. I know I should be embarrassed. I know I should be ashamed that someone has caught us like this but I'm not. I want them to see. Something inside me wants everyone to see that this man, this king of our city wants me of all people.

I start gyrating my hips, riding his fingers and Nico turns to watch me curiously.

"We have an update." Preston says pointedly.

Nico snarls and then his fingers are out. I'm no longer his focus and I look away annoyed but understanding. I wrap my robe back around. I don't want Preston to see me now. Nico steps back, making a play of licking his fingers for us both to see.

Preston clears his throat but apart from that he makes no comment.

"What's the update?" Nico asks turning away from me to where he's already laying something out on the island with the row of bar stools.

He looks at me and then Nico glances too.

"Do you want me to go?" I say.

Nico pulls a face like he's not sure.

"It's okay. I'll be outside on the balcony." I say before he needs to. There's clearly something going off and I don't want to distract him but more than that I don't want to cause more issues. I want him to understand that I'm not the kind of person who takes offence so easily as that. I'm not high maintenance. If anything

I'm probably too much of a people pleaser but I guess we all have our vices.

I walk over to the huge bi-folds. I don't even know where the door bit is so I try one end but it doesn't budge.

"Like this." Nico says behind me and I gasp because he's done it again. He's snuck up on me.

He opens the door and I murmur my thanks.

As I step out I can tell he's still watching me so I make a point of not looking back. Of focusing on exploring this new space only all I can focus on is the view. We're in the hills. The main city is below us. This is the most sought after area to live. The most exclusive. I've never even set foot in this part before though it makes sense that Nico would be here. That his home would be here.

I breathe in the air and for once it's not thick with exhaust fumes and dirt. It's clear. Clean. I can smell the nearby trees and pollen from flowers in the garden below. It feels like I'm in paradise, the very gardens of Eden itself.

It's mad to be here. To be propelled into this world but I decide in this moment I will do everything in my power to please Nico. To keep him happy. To be by his side because this world of his, this place is everything a girl could dream of, but more than that, Nico is everything I didn't know I wanted in a man. Everything I need too.

Him

CHAPTER
Eleven

I watch her for a few moments. She's staring out at the view as if she can't quite believe it's eyes.

I like it and I hate it too. The look of surprise on her face is something that makes my dick throb. But this place, this house, all of this shouldn't feel so alien to her. Her life till now shouldn't have been so shit that this feels like a luxury in comparison.

"Are you going to watch her all day?" Preston asks and I smirk.

"Fuck off." I say turning around and leaving her to it. "So what do we have?"

"We've tracked the vans. They went to a warehouse the other side of the city. We think that's where they've taken the stuff."

"Think?" I reply.

"We're sending some scouts in. Nothing that will alert them."

"Who?"

"Couple of street kids."

I pull a face. I don't like using kids. If shit goes down I don't want a child's blood on my hands. Adults can consent. Kids don't understand what the fuck they're getting into.

"It makes sense." Preston states. Yeah it does but that doesn't mean I have to like it.

"What do you want to do when once we confirm it's there?" He asks.

"Leave it."

"What?"

I grin. I've planned this all out. Every last detail. "It stays where it is. I want them to be oblivious. I want Emerson to be oblivious. To think he's outwitted me."

He nods like he understands. Only he doesn't. No one does. That's why I'm so successful. I outmanoeuvre them. I outthink them. I think in ways none of them are capable of and that is why I will win this new war before it even gets started.

"And the girl?" He asks.

"What about her?"

"Is she involved?"

"In what?" I narrow my eyes.

"This plan of yours." He states.

"She has nothing to do with this."

"That's not what I meant."

"What did you mean then?"

"It just seems convenient that you've suddenly taken an interest in her after how long of her working at the bar…?"

"Six months." I cut across.

"Six months." He repeats.

"That girl is mine." I say. "She's always been mine. It's not a sudden interest, I have watched her for the last two years. Helped her. Taken care of her. Though she doesn't have a clue."

He frowns for a moment and then I see the penny drop. "The medical bills." He says and I nod.

Eleri thinks she was receiving money from a grant. A fund set up by this city to help the poor who need lifesaving treatment but can't afford it. But that's not the case. I pay her bills. I pay for the security she doesn't know surrounds her shitty apartment, who follow her around unseen to make sure no one else lays a hand on her.

I keep her safe. It's what a man does. He takes care of his woman and she is mine.

"Who the fuck is she?" Preston asks leaning over the island at me.

"She's mine. That's all you need to know." I reply. I can't explain anymore because that's the only way I can explain it, define it too. She's mine. It's that simple. I need her the same way I need blood in my veins, air in my lungs, food in belly. I need her with me, beside me, a part of me, because now that I've claimed her, tasted her, let her into my life, if I lose her now the world will hold nothing for me.

"And this man?" Preston says bringing me out of my thoughts because I've somehow been staring at her again through the glass. Admiring the way the wind blows against the robe she has on and the outline of her arse cheeks are there for me to see. For me to hunger for.

"Huh?"

"This man. Is he connected to Emerson?" Preston says.

I look down and it's a copy of the photo Eleri gave me.

"Where did you get that?" I ask.

"Blaine. He's got some men looking for him."

I nod. "I know. I told him to."

"Who is he?"

I glance at Eleri again. I can't help it. My dick is still hard. Preston is doing his best not to look at it but I'm so close to telling him to fuck off so I can turn my attention back to the woman I'm aching to fuck.

"It was him wasn't it?" Preston says.

"Yes." I reply. "He was the ring leader. But there were others. Three others. I don't know their names or their faces but I want them all found. I want them all taken to the crypt and Eleri will watch as I make them pay."

Preston nods. His face looks pale though because we both know what the crypt means but he also looks like he would do the same in my situation. They marked my woman. They touched her. Hurt her. Tried to destroy her beauty because she rejected them. They deserve to suffer. They deserve to die for that.

Preston looks out the glass, at Eleri. "If you want to avoid another incident like earlier I suggest you make sure everyone knows who she is." He says.

I grunt in reply. I don't need advice from him. Not when it comes to taking care of her.

He leaves and I stay, leaning over the island watching her for a few moments more. Only I think she knows I'm watching because she bends over the glass balustrade, making a point of looking at something below her and all I can see is her perfect round ass positioned at such an angle it would be so easy to rip that fabric up and sink my cock hard into her with her wriggling body beneath me.

I groan. My queen is toying with me I realise. And I'm done watching.

I let the door slam as I shut it and she lifts her head to look at me. She's still bent over though, from the angle she's at anyone in the garden is getting a perfect view of her tits.

"You took your time." She teases and I smirk.

"Did you miss me that much?"

She bites her lip. Of course she fucking did.

I walk up to her and my hands are on her hips, keeping her in place as she tries to move. My dick is shoved right in between those chunky delicious ass cheeks of hers and I let her feel for a moment how hard I still am.

"Are you going to fuck me now?" She says.

"No."

She lets out a sigh and if I'm honest it amuses me. How the tables have turned. How much she wants me now. How desperate she is for my cock.

I pull the robe up and the satin slip with it, exposing her skin to the cool spring breeze. She shudders and her smooth skin erupts into goosebumps.

"Did you like riding my fingers for Preston to see?" I ask her, staring at where her ass hole is presented like a treat with her already dripping cunt just below.

She nods. "I wanted him to know." She replies.

"Know what?" I ask.

"That you want me. I want everyone to know."

I grin. Fuck this girl is so mine. I glance around and I can see my men, my guards on the peripheries. I grab her hair yanking her head at an angle so that she can see them too.

"Do you want them to know as well?" I ask.

"Yes." She says. And then she says it again as I plunge my fingers in between her slick, wet folds. "Yes."

"Yes you do." I say. "Because under that shy façade you're a greedy little slut aren't you?"

She nods, her head moving only as much as I allow it.

"For you." She breathes.

"My greedy little slut." I agree.

I'm finger fucking her hard now, relentlessly. All my pent up frustration, all my tiredness, all my anger at not being able to start this off right between us is being channelled into her warm, dripping cunt.

And by god does she love it. She rocks her hips, she encourages me. I think my nails might be tearing at the soft flesh of her insides but she doesn't seem to care. She said before she wants me to use her and right now that's what it feels like I'm doing, she's my stress relief.

My toy to use as I please.

The thought comes into my head and while it turns me on it annoys me too because I don't see her as that. She's not just a thing to be fucked. She's mine. My woman. And I'll treat her right, starting with her cuming here, on my balcony for every one of my staff to witness.

She lets out a loud moan. A cry of pure ecstasy and I latch onto it.

"The louder you scream the more people will know." I growl into her ear as she pushes back, pushes my fingers into her harder and harder. I can feel her muscles tensing. I can feel her body right on the point of release.

My queen, my wanton angel is about to fall and I am the devil bringing her down.

She shudders, hot liquid leaks out, down my wrist, down my arm. She's so messy when she cums. That's how I know she will squirt properly.

And then she's screaming, singing, crying out as loud as her lungs will let her. My men look then. Everyone looks and I pull her head higher for them to see. I want them to know too. I want them all to see my queen and what she does to me. I want them to witness her triumph right here, on this balcony in front of the whole god damn city.

As she hangs panting over the glass, I go on my knees and lick her clean. She quivers under the feel of my tongue on her flushed lips and her legs jerk a little.

I keep my hands on her ass though, enjoying the feel of her curves as I hold her in place for me. I don't know if my men are watching now. I don't really care.

This is about her. My woman. About sating her needs. At least, sating them enough for now.

"Is that what you wanted?" I ask.

She moans in response. Yeah, it was.

I let her slide down the glass and catch her body as she drops to the decking.

My hands instinctively find her breasts and I play with her nipples as she leans back, letting me expose her more.

"You're my little slut aren't you?" I say as I feel them harden for me.

"Yes." She says.

I kiss the side of her head, the side without the scar. "My queen too." I say.

"Does that make you the king?" She gasps.

"Your king." I agree.

She moans again and her hand reaches behind to grab my dick. "Will you let your queen service you then?" She says.

Now how can I refuse an offer like that?

Her

CHAPTER
Twelve

His dick has been calling out, from the minute we were in the kitchen I could feel how much he needed his balls to empty. How much he wanted me to empty them. And then Preston came and he got distracted.

And then he got more distracted with how I was presenting myself, hoping he might take the bait and finally fuck me.

But now it's my turn. My opportunity to show him that I want his cock just as much as I did the first time, hell I want it more now. Now that I've cum twice for him, I want him more than is reasonable, more than is sane.

My hand is rubbing against him through the fabric. His cock is just so big it's hard to even get a grip. Maybe it's a good thing he's taking his time because he seems more than a little obsessed with my body and if he wanted to just fuck me all the time he could do some serious damage to my insides.

I twist around. I want to see him, to see the look on his face as I pleasure him.

He takes the opportunity to move too and suddenly he's on his feet, pulling me up and he carries me to where a table is and lays me out flat. I frown confused because this is meant to be about him, his release.

And then he moves to where my head is and yanks his throbbing, veiny, divine cock out.

I grin licking my lips as I realise what he wants. He wants me to suck him off again. From this angle though there will be no holding back and I can see from his face that's what he intends.

I glance around. Are his men still watching? God I hope so. I want them to see. I want Preston and that Blaine guy to see to as I take Nico's cock in my throat.

I tilt my head back, right off the edge, opening my mouth and use my hands to guide him closer but he's in control. Even now, even when I'm the one granting the pleasure, he's the one making the big moves.

"Take my cock Eleri. Take it all." He says sliding into me.

My eye widens as he pushes inch by inch into my mouth. He feels even bigger this time, as if the need has made his dick swell to impossible proportions. I can feel my spit already sliding down my face.

I don't want to gag. I don't want to choke.

I want everyone to see me sucking Nico's ten inch dick off and taking every bit without complaint.

He groans, picking up pace. His balls are slapping into my face. His dick is past my tonsils, down my throat. I can taste him in every cell of my body. I'm fighting my gag reflex so hard and my face is screwed up tight with the effort.

"Relax." He says as if he can feel my tension.

I murmur in response but his dick is preventing me from speaking so all it results in is some low vibration against him.

He groans, sliding a hand down between my breasts and then he massages them, manipulates them, rolls my nipples as I focusing on sucking.

"That's a good girl." He says. "You're doing so good."

I move my hand, I don't realise I'm doing it but I'm touching myself, teasing my clit and he groans in approval. I know he liked watching me on the camera so I know it'll turn him on more to see it in reality.

"Yes my queen." He say, bucking his hips harder. I can hear he's close now. I can feel his pace is becoming relentless. I'm starting to choke again, starting to feel his dick catch every time he rocks into me.

He grabs my hand, the one that's been masturbating myself and he sucks on my fingers, twisting his tongue over the digits to lick up my juices.

And then he lets out a half roar as he cums. His seed is so warm as it pours down my throat and I swallow over and over, trying not to choke on it.

He pulls his dick out and I half cough, rolling onto my side. It's not the ending I was after but he looks happy. Fuck, he looks like a king that just got his throne.

"You take my cock so well." He says.

"I think I just need more practice." I say wiping the mix of cum and saliva that's dripped down my chin.

He laughs. "We can certainly arrange that."

CHAPTER

Thirteen

She's been here for almost week now.

At every opportunity I'm grabbing her, touching her, feeling her breasts and that fan-fucking-tastic ass. If I'd known she'd feel as good as she does I would have made my moves sooner.

Hell, I might even have brought her here after she left the hospital. Played Florence Nightingale and nursed her back to health with my cock.

But it wouldn't have worked.

I know that. I know as much as we're enjoying our time, this girl has trust issues, unsurprising trust issues and that's another reason I'm not fucking her just yet. Because as much as I worship her body, as much as I cannot get enough, I want her to know I see her for more than how she looks. I see her for who she is. And who she will be.

Afterall if it's just about her physical traits I'd be no different to the brutes who maimed her. Not really anyway. Because that's all they saw. Big tits, big ass, curves to die for and when she turned them down, they thought they had the right to destroy her. As if anyone has that right.

My divine sleeping beauty.

I stroke her hair. She's gotten used to me perving over her now. She's gotten used to me staring at her face, refusing to be cowed by the scarring there.

For the last few days though things have been ramping up. Building.

I've had to spend more time away from her than I wanted. But she doesn't seem to mind. Doesn't complain. My woman understands my time is precious and she seems grateful for any attention I give her.

I watch her through the feed, watch as she sits with Sarpedon wrapped around her, as she showers, as she keeps herself busy while I am occupied with meetings, strategizing, planning. If everything goes accordingly this war will be over soon enough and I can focus all my efforts on ensuring Eleri is happy.

She rolls over looking up at me and a small, almost bashful smile creeps across her lips.

"Good morning." I say.

She takes in my shirt, my suit, the fact that I'm already dressed. "You have to go." She says and I nod. "Why didn't you wake me sooner?"

"You looked too peaceful to wake." I say.

She rolls her eye. We've fitted into a comfortable existence, the two of us. And day by day she's becoming more herself. More confident. More sassy too.

I stroke her cheek and she winces. "Why do you do that?" She asks.

"Do what?"

"Touch it."

I pause for a moment. She means her scar. "I don't know." I admit.

"It doesn't disgust you?" She says.

"Why would it?"

"Because it's ugly. I'm ugly." She states.

"No you're not." I growl.

She looks away for a moment and my anger flares.

"You are not ugly. And neither is that scar."

She snorts. "That's a lie."

"Eleri, those men tried to make you ugly. To destroy your beauty because they couldn't enjoy it themselves."

She nods and then looks up at me, tilting her head. "How do you know it was more than just him?" She asks.

Shit. I open my mouth to reply and my phone goes off. Saved by the bell I guess.

"I'm sorry, I have to take this." I say.

"Go." She replies like we're not in the middle of something. Like I've not just revealed something fucking massive. She's not a drama queen, she doesn't mind that I'm treating her like she's not my priority despite the fact that she should be.

I nod and leave her to it, hating it all the same.

Preston is waiting for me when I get outside. Blaine is already there.

We drive in silence. My men are on edge. Alert. In truth they have nothing to be concerned about but I like that they're wary. It gives them an edge. It means they're prepared and we won't end up caught with our trousers down and our dicks out.

The cars screech to a halt. My men get out first. Then Preston. Then me.

I walk in last. Not for dramatic effect, but because I'm still processing this. Still mulling this over. I can play this two ways.

I glance at Preston. I know the way he'd advocate. He'd go for the safe option. The easier option. He'd say play the long game. Play the clever game. But I'm done playing. And I'm done waiting too.

I walk into the dimly lit space. Blaine is there, arms crossed, usual smug look on his face.

In front of him is a middle aged man, chained up, hanging from the ceiling. I can see Blaine's already had some fun.

"Well?" I say.

"He's said some shit. Nothing we don't already know." Blaine replies.

I tilt my head, looking at the man who once I would have considered a father figure. Before he betrayed me the first time.

"Nico." He gasps my name and blood splutters from his lips. Clearly Blaine gave him a good beating.

"You're working for them." I say.

He shakes his head. "I'm not. I promise. I've never betrayed you." Like he can just pretend the last time didn't happen.

"We found this on him." Blaine cuts across nodding his head for one of the men to hold out whatever it is.

I narrow my eyes taking the phone, flicking through the messages he should have deleted. I guess I should be happy the man is such an imbecile that his own ineptitude is what will hang him.

"How do you explain that then?" I ask flashing the screen before his face.

"I…" He splutters knowing the game is up. "I'll tell you everything. I'll tell you all I know." He says.

I snarl. This man has tried to play me so many times.

"Nico." Preston says quietly.

"What?" I snap.

"I think we should hear what he has to say."

He's right. I know he is. Though I doubt Matuso has anything worth hearing we have to listen anyway."

"Talk." I say turning back to him.

He nods. "I loved your mother..."

"Not about that." I snap. "I want to hear plans. I want to hear evidence. I want to know exactly what they're up to."

He nods furiously so. And then he talks. He talks so much. He doesn't shut up.

And when he's done, when there's finally nothing but dull silence in the air I see that hopeful look in his eyes. He thinks he's saved himself. He thinks I will forgive. That I will forget. Only I did that once before and look where it got me.

Blaine smirks. His gold teeth flash in the dull light.

I pull my gun. I could have one of my men do it. I could have them drown him, poison him, hell even beat him to death if I chose but Matuso betrayed me. Betrayed my mother too. It's only right he dies by my hand.

I raise my gun, click off the safety, and pull the trigger.

The noise echoes around us. The bang reverberates in my ears.

Preston mutters something and I know what he's thinking. That I should have waited. That I should have spared him until my brother was dealt with but I'm done being betrayed and I'm done turning a blind eye to it.

Blaine claps. His hands coming together loudly and a few of the men shift. They're not all comfortable with Blaine's particular brand of justice. The man's a sociopath. We all know it but that's why I employ him.

We can't all play nice and with Blaine on my side it makes sure this city knows I'm not someone to be trifled with. Or at least it did until my brother came back to town.

Her

CHAPTER
Fourteen

He's been gone all day. The same as yesterday.

I make sure not to complain. As much as I miss him I know he has more going on than just me. So I spend the day baking. I've never been that much of a baker but I can follow a recipe well enough.

I make chocolate chip cookies first. They're not bad, though they're a little undercooked. I make a point of offering them to all the men, all the guards that seem to loiter in the downstairs space. They take them greedily and thank me. I like the fact they're not afraid of me, that me fucking their boss, being with their boss doesn't mean they're scared of even looking at me wrong.

I make muffins next. And then I remember that I hate making muffins, so I scrap it half way and repurpose the dough into a sort of cake thing that again I offer to the guards when it's cool enough. I think I might be fattening them up to much but they don't object.

When I'm bored of that I go and sit out one of the balconies, and let the warmth of the spring sun soak into my skin while Sarpedon stretches out clearly enjoying it too. I'm half tempted to swim. But I don't have the nerve to show so much skin without Nico here.

Since being here I think my confidence has grown. I'm no longer draping my body in baggy clothes. Hiding myself from everyone's gaze. Nico likes dresses, judging by all the slinky things he's stuffed my wardrobe with. He likes me to wear things that show off my body, accentuate my curves. Clothes that even a month ago I would have shied away from for fear of the repercussions.

But with Nico I'm not so afraid. No one would dare touch me while I'm with him. No one dare lay a finger on me and that thought alone makes me feel things I shouldn't.

I know he won't hurt me. At least not like that. Because I've asked him to fuck me so many times now, practically begged the man and yet he won't. Not that he's adverse to touching me, hell he practically worships my body but as yet he still hasn't given me the pleasure of his cock inside me and I'm actually aching with the constant want for it.

Perhaps that's his plan. To get me so wet, to get me so desperate that when he does finally do it I fall head over heels, lost in everything he is bestowing on me. It certainly wouldn't be a bad plan.

Hell, I think I'm already falling head over heels for him and it still feels like we've only just gotten started.

I sigh getting to my feet and delicately pick Sarpedon up , carrying him back to his ginormous enclosure. Nico wasn't lying when he said he'd had a bigger one made, it's enough for a snake twice Sarpedon's size. And I'll admit I feel a burst of something every time I see it. Sarpedon slithers away, over the rocks, to a new favourite hiding space. If I could I would have left him to sunbathe but the creature is an escape artist worthy of Houdini himself and though I know he's not necessarily looking for a life of freedom, I doubt he'd turn down the opportunity if it presented itself.

I watch him for a few moments more. He's due to shed soon. I used to collect his old skin, turn it into bits of art. I wonder what Nico would think if I started doing that again. Would he think me mad? Would he change his mind entirely?

He'll be back soon I tell myself and I want to make sure I'm ready and waiting for him. But as I make my way through the house something feels different. Something feels off.

I pause, feeling the hairs on the back of my neck standing up. It's like a sixth sense, a premonition of some shit that's about to happen and I turn around to grab my phone wanting, needing to speak to Nico.

Only something grabs me. Someone grabs me.

I cry out as I'm pushed to the ground. Someone is wrenching my arms behind my back, tying them so tightly with something that half rips into my skin.

And then I'm dragged, through the house, through the front door and thrown into the back of a van before it speeds away.

Him

CHAPTER
Fifteen

The front door is open. The house is empty. Half my men are dead but more than that, all I can focus on is the fact that Eleri is not here.

"What the fuck happened?" I ask.

"Apparently while we were busy making moves your brother made a few of his own." Preston says like it's not fucking obvious.

I walk into the house. There's a strange mix of death and cookies in the air. I wrinkle my nose in confusion.

"Down here." Someone calls I move, down into the lower recesses, seeing my men, seeing them piled up, one on top of the other. All dead, or as close to it as one can be.

"Get the medics in here." I say. If there's any chance these men will live then I'm willing to pay. They're loyal to me. They risk their lives for me. It's only right I do the same for them too.

I turn around and take the stairs two at a time. I can smell more baking. I think it's Eleri. She seems to enjoy cooking more than I realised and the smell of it in the air is like a constant reminder that I haven't found her. That she's not in my arms.

I walk into our room. Our bedroom. I'm met with nothing but silence. Stale. Stagnant silence.

"Eleri." I call her name. I don't expect a reply but some small part of me is wanting it anyway.

They've trashed my place, sprayed it with graffiti. Smeared excrement on the walls. Most of our clothes have been thrown into the bath and burnt. If Eleri wasn't gone and my men weren't dead it would be comical.

It's like a five year old having a paddy. But that's my brother all over.

Preston appears and I realise he's got her snake in his arms. He looks uncomfortable, as if the creature might turn around and bite him but Sarpedon looks mellow enough. I feel a fleeting sense of relief that they hadn't killed it but it's another reminder of who is missing.

"We've got new footage." Blaine says storming up to me. We knew before we got here that some shit had gone down. I just didn't realise to what extent.

"Show me." I say.

Blaine passes the tablet over and I stare at the screen. It's the same van's we caught on the hidden surveillance cameras. They're driving so boringly no one would even notice them. They're in the city. The industrial part.

I know she's in one of them. My gut tells me so.

I curl my hands into fists.

If they've hurt her, if they've even thought to touch her I'm going to flay them alive.

"Get me a location. I want to know where they're headed. I want to know where they took her and I want to know it now." I bellow.

CHAPTER
Sixteen

I don't know where I am.

They've put something over my head like a sack. It's cold. And it's quiet. Horribly so.

Someone shoved me on a chair and I guess I should be grateful I'm not forced to lie on the freezing concrete that even now is soaking the warmth from my feet.

A door opens. I know it's for this room. This place I'm in and I whimper before I can stop myself.

"This is her?" Someone says and someone else grunts.

They're standing over me now. I can sense them. I can hear their breathing.

One of them grabs my head wrenching it back through the fabric sack.

"I wouldn't bother removing it." The other man says. "Apparently her face is all fucked up."

The man holding me snorts. "So what's he see in her then?"

"Fuck knows but her body's decent enough."

The man holding me takes the opportunity to grope my left breast hard and grunts in agreement.

I screw my face up. I know they can't see me. I know they wouldn't care if they could but I'm petrified. All my confidence, all my belief that Nico would protect me is starting to come crashing down like a house of cards. Was I an idiot? Was I stupid to put my faith in him, a man I hardly know, in truth a man I've already given far too much to. I should have known better, I mean has history not shown me enough times what happens when I ignore my instincts?

I'm forced up, out of the chair and made to walk

I don't know where they're taking me now but every step fills me with dread and I try to stop it, trying to stop moving but my legs are kicked out from under me and I'm dragged. The floor cuts into my shins, into my skin and I bite my lip hard to not give them any satisfaction of hearing me cry.

I'm in a new room.

It's warmer. All I can hear are the two men's breathing and my own.

A hand gropes me. Another starts peeling away my clothes. I know what's happening. What they're going to do. I'm not an idiot and I cry out, trying to get them off me but it's no good. My hands are tied and besides it's two against one. I don't stand a chance.

Rough calloused hands run over my skin. It feels so different from how Nico touches me. These men aren't doing it out of pleasure.

It's a control thing.

A dominance thing.

Just like the men from the alley.

I whimper again as one of them twists my nipple so hard I think it might rip.

"She's got curves alright." He says as I squirm desperately trying to get away.

"Let's find out what her cunt feels like." The other says and I hear his belt being undone. I fight harder then. I kick out. I try to punch the man behind me with my arms but I can't even get any movement.

They laugh and I'm pulled back, pulled to sit on one of them. I can feel his dick against my ass. The prick is hard. This is turning him on.

"Spread her legs, hold her for me." The other says and the man I'm sat on wraps his boots around both my feet, yanking them apart.

I'm still in my panties. Somehow they've forgotten to remove them in their haste to violate me thus far but I guess it won't take much for them to rectify that.

As the other man steps closer and my fear lurches to an uncontrollable level, a door opens, and it feels like the whole atmosphere changes.

They both still.

They're like statues now. Frozen to the spot. I can sense their fear. I can smell it and it makes me more afraid because if they're shitting themselves then I'm in even more danger.

Someone walks in. No, more than one person.

I hear boots. At least half a dozen of them, meaning there's three new men in this room. Three new men with me half naked, bound, straddling a man who has every intention of raping me.

The sack comes off. My hair falls to cover my face as it does and a hand sweeps it back.

I look up.

I can't help it. I have to look and I see him staring back at me.

CHAPTER

Seventeen

They've stripped her. They've tied her up. She's sat right now on one of their fucking laps with her body exposed for them both. How I haven't killed them already I don't know but my concern is for her. For my woman who they've had the audacity to take, the audacity to touch.

She's staring at me in shock, in shame, in relief too.

She knows I've come to rescue her. And that these arseholes will pay for what they've done.

I want to cover her. To wrap her in my arms but she's sat patiently, obediently waiting for me to tell her what to do as if she'd not surrounded by half a dozen men right now.

I look at the man holding her, the man who even now has his boots keeping her legs apart. He smirks. The stupid fuck has the balls to smirk. My anger flares. I see red and I raise my gun, pulling the trigger. Blasting his fucking head off.

Blood splatters. His head practically explodes and my angel is covered in it.

I look at her expecting to see shock. Expecting to see horror but that's not what's there.

She's smiling just enough to show me she approves. She wanted me to kill him. She wanted him to pay.

I pull her off him. Pull her body to me and Preston cuts the ties holding her wrists. As soon as she's free she reaches for my gun in my other hand. I raise an eyebrow but I don't stop her. She clearly wants to do something and I'm not going to get in her way.

She turns, staring at the other man, the one with his cock out. The one who no doubt moments earlier was planning on violating my woman. She raises the gun and he's the one begging now. Shaking his head, pleading for mercy. She tilts her head, points it at his chest and pulls the trigger just like I did.

My perfect fucking queen.

"Eleri." I murmur and she turns passing the gun to Preston without looking at him.

"You came." It's all she says before her lips crash into mine and I'm pulling her in tighter, wrapping my arms around her, feeling her hunger and her fear and every other emotion pulsing through her body right now.

She's covered in blood, covered in dirt, but in this moment she's never looked more incredible.

And I've never wanted her more.

She's rocking her hips against me, gyrating, and fuck I can't say no. I won't say no either.

My men get the hint and fuck off. All of them quickly exiting the room. They've got shit to do anyway. There's others to take care of. More trash to take out if you will.

But right now I need to take care of Eleri.

I kiss her neck, I lick at the blood covering her skin. She moans as I do it and I take my time, licking, swiping, marking her body with saliva and removing the last traces of that man.

"Did they hurt you?" I ask between licks.

"No. You got here right when I needed you."

I grunt. That's not exactly true. She needed me back at the house. Back when they decided to raid it, killing half my guards and taking her in the process.

"Stop thinking." She says grabbing my face to make me look at her. "Stop replaying it."

"It shouldn't have happened."

"No, but we'll make them pay." She says speaking like a true queen.

Her hands are on my belt, undoing it clumsily but she gets it off, and then she's freeing my cock which of course is hard and throbbing for her.

"Take me." She says. "Fuck me. Claim me."

"Here?" I say. It's not the setting I had envisioned for our first time.

"Here." She says grinning. Her skin is still speckled with blood. Her nipples are so hard right now I think they could cut glass.

I'd planned on lubing up, on smothering us both because I know how big my cock is and I know how much it can hurt but there's none here. I have to go in raw and hope she's aroused enough and wet enough inside not to tear.

She pulls her panties off and like a red flag to a bull I make my move, picking her up and she wraps her legs around my waist, letting me guide her down onto me.

My cock is nudging at her entrance. I've not even touched her cunt and I can feel she's dripping. Good, she'll need all the juices she has to get me in and for it not to hurt. She moans as I push inside just a bit. Her muscles, her flesh, her perfect body adjusts to fit my girth but I can see it's not all that comfortable.

"I'll go slow." I say.

"No you won't." She says back, gripping my shirt, half glaring at me. "This body is yours. I am yours. You are going to mould me to fit you."

"Eleri…"

"Fuck me Nico. Fuck me hard and fuck me like I need you to." I grin. I can hear it in her voice. She's serious. My devil spawn. My wanton little whore is back and I'm ready to fulfil her needs.

"Then take your throne my queen." I say as I shove the rest of my length inside her hard and she cries out in shock and pain. I pull out, slowly, hoping her juices have coated me enough and I plunge back inside her.

Fuck she feels so good. Her cunt is gripping me so tightly, her nails are digging in, I can feel the warmth of her, the way her arousal is already coating us. She wants this, she's enjoying this. Enjoying me fucking her.

I pick up my pace. She said hard and by god that's what I'm going to give her now. She starts grunting, writhing, rocking her hips and her tits bounce with every move she makes. My majestic queen, my warrior, my perfect angel, fucking me back as I fuck her.

"You like the feel of my cock?" I say as she throws her head back.

"Yes." She screams loud enough for everyone in this piece of shit place to hear.

"You like your throne?" I say and she nods. Of course she does. This woman was made for me. Made for my cock. Made for my pleasure. Just as I was made for hers.

"Cum in me. Mark my insides. Tear me apart." She cries and I realise it's still hurting her, still painful but she's enjoying it all the same. Maybe she's a masochist. Maybe my little slut is into more than I realised.

I grab her tit, raising it, and suck hard on her nipple.

She moans more. Her body is so responsive. Every touch I make, everything I do seems to elicit a response that's salacious, wanton, but necessary.

She runs her nails down my back, scrapes at my flesh and I groan. I want her to mark me too. I want us both to bear evidence of this.

Her walls are clenching, her body is starting to lose control and my dick is moments from release.

"Cum with me Eleri." I order.

She nods, giving in as if she's in control and her body latches onto my cock tighter. I growl out in response, my dick pouring out as she screams and screams and screams.

My perfect fucking angel is being filled, is milking my cock right now of every last drop and as my mouth finds hers I know from now on I'm going to be fucking her till she can't take it anymore.

CHAPTER
Eighteen

I'm wearing his jacket because I can't bear the thought of putting any of my own clothes back on. I'm only wearing my panties because I need something to catch all the cum that he's filled me with. We're not going back to the house. He's taking me to a hotel. His hotel. The best hotel in the damn city.

I let out a little chuckle at the thought of me walking barefoot into such a place.

"What's so funny?" Nico asks me coming out from wherever his head has been for the last few minutes.

"I'm just imagining the shocked look on everyone's face when I step out wearing nothing but your jacket with your cum smeared down my thighs."

He grins. "Let them stare. There's fuck all they can do about it."

I smile back. A month ago I would have panicked at the very idea of this, of being the centre of attention but with Nico beside me, with him holding my hand I don't give a fuck what anyone else thinks.

We pull up outside. A man opens the door and Nico gets out before offering me his hand like the perfect gentleman. Tossing my hair back I figure there's only one way to play this now and I steel myself for what's about to happen as I step out under the gaze of what feels like the entire city's elite.

No one talks. No one dares say a thing as we walk inside the marble wonder that is the lobby. People are queuing for the front desk. Others are sat having drinks in the decadently styled bar.

Nico leads me past everyone. The way his jacket hangs make it look like some statement dress with my cleavage on almost full display. The only thing that ruins the look is the lack of heels but I guess beggars can't be choosers.

He guides me to the elevator, ignoring the front desk entirely and as the doors slowly glide shut I can feel everyone staring.

Nico smirks, more at the look on my face than at these people's response.

The elevator shoots upwards and my ears pop with the speed as we gain height. When it finally pings for the penthouse I'm met with the most breath-taking view and I swear my jaw drops.

"It's not bad is it?" Nico says.

"Not bad?" I gasp stepping out, feeling the warmth of the underfloor heating already soaking into my feet. I walk over to where the huge glass separates us from the beautiful parkland and the city below and press my face into it. "This place is incredible."

"This is my second home. And now your home." He says. "Let me show you around."

It's not as big as his house but it's still incredible. It's designed like a duplex with three bedrooms on the higher floors each with their own dedicated bathrooms and walk-in wardrobes.

On the first floor there's a cinema room, a sitting room, a kitchen and a dining room.

Nico's had a new enclosure brought here for Sarpedon and he's already exploring it. I feel relief that he wasn't harmed, that those arseholes didn't do anything to hurt him but I also feel guilty that he's gone through so much upheaval but he doesn't seem all that effected. I'm not sure how we're going to store his food though but I guess that's a problem for later. He got fed yesterday so he won't be all that hungry yet.

Nico points to two doors, one on either side, of the long entrance hall which connect to two additional suites.

"My men are in there. No one will get near you again." He says.

I nod. I know he thinks he let me down but I don't agree. Besides after the way he rescued me, the way he shot that man, I think he more than made up for it.

"Are you hungry?" He asks.

"Starving." I say. Somehow I'm always ravenous around this man. Ravenous for food and ravenous for him too.

He laughs as if he can tell. "How about we order some room service then?"

"How long will it take?" I ask.

He shrugs. "Maybe half an hour at the most."

"So long enough to show my gratitude." I reply dropping to my knees.

His eyebrows raise. "I think you did that already." He says but my hands are already undoing his belt, dropping his trousers and I'm reaching for his cock which even now is coming so readily to life.

"How about I show you some more?" I say.

"What my queen wants, my queen gets." He says before half groaning as I run my tongue up the side of his shaft. His dick jerks as I do it. He's still only semi-hard but that's okay, I'm more than happy to work with what I have.

I push him back onto the leather seat and he doesn't put up a fight but he does reach for the phone and dials for food.

I fondle his balls, lick along him more, swirl my tongue over the very top as he tries to order. I'm deliberately teasing him, enjoying the effects of how my tongue is tantalising him. It's hard not to laugh as he stumbles on his words, as his voice slurs, as he groans.

I don't care what he's actually ordering. I'd eat anything but right now what I want most is his dick in my mouth.

He puts the phone down, drops it, and turns his full attention on me.

I think I enjoy seeing the look on his face almost as much as the feel of it as when he slides between my lips. He looks like all his Christmases have come at once. He looks like he's been bestowed every gift possible by god. And the way he groans, it's like heaven to my ears and part of me wants to record it and play it every time I touch myself.

I want to cum only to that sound.

I want to die to it ringing in my ears.

"Eleri." He murmurs. I feel myself getting wetter as he utters my name. I'm still a sticky mess from earlier, I can smell his cum on me, but I don't care because Nico doesn't seem to either.

He tucks his hands behind his head, thrusting his hips forward, letting me take full charge. Full command of his body.

I lean over him. His dick is at full throttle now and I plunge him into my mouth properly.

"Fuck." He growls.

I pull him out with popping sound.

"Are you enjoying your thank you?" I say.

He nods. "So much."

I grin, taking hold of him and swirl my tongue around him more. His precum is on my lips, on my tastebuds. This man's cock feels like my sole obsession now.

He starts thrusting more, and with every push he hits hard into the back of my throat. I guess I'm starting to get used to it though because I'm not choking as much I did the last time.

Vaguely I register a pinging sound and Nico looks around seeing someone bringing the food.

He points roughly to where he wants it and I feel the man's wide eyes on me as I continue to suck Nico off. I half grin at him. I don't care what he thinks. All I care about is Nico and his pleasure in this moment.

"You're so good at this." Nico groans. Clearly he doesn't care if the man is there either.

I fondle his balls again. Massage them. I can feel them tightening. I can feel his thrusts becoming more erratic. He's got good timing considering our dinner just arrived but I want to make sure we both enjoy our starter first. His hands fall on my head. He starts pounding, fucking my face harder and then he cums. And that same delicious saltiness pours down my throat as I relish every drop.

He falls back into the chair. Staring at me.

I grin at him, remaining on my knees, trying to figure out what he's thinking right now as I wipe my mouth.

"You're incredible." He says.

I laugh. "No. You are."

He shakes his head sitting up, and adjusts his pants before holding his hand for me to take. "My dream woman."

"Your dream whore more like." I murmur.

"If you're happy to be my whore, I'm happy to keep your mouth occupied." He says.

"Then fill it whenever you want." I say biting my lip.

He laughs, leading me over to where the food was hastily left along with a magnum of champagne chilling in an ice-bucket.

I pull it out looking at him almost questioningly. "What are we celebrating?" I ask.

"Me finally fucking you." He replies.

"You say that like I've been the one putting you off." I state.

He raises an eyebrow before sitting down and tucking in. I take the hint to shut up and join him.

Him

CHAPTER
Nineteen

I run her a bath. It seems like the gentlemanly thing to do. Though in truth all I really want to do is fuck her again.

But she needs to wash. We both need to wash.

She's still got blood on her. And I can smell my cum between her thighs. She lets me lead her up the stairs and there's the hint of a grin on her face. She slides my jacket from her shoulders as I sit on the stool admiring her.

She steps into the shower first, washing off the blood and the dirt and then she makes a play of massaging her breasts with the shower gel.

My mouth waters as she does it. She squeezes her nipples, rolls them between her thumbs. She doesn't even have to try to be sexual, she just is. Every cell in her body oozes with it.

I strip my clothes off when I can't take any more but she slips past me grinning before sliding into the bath. Now she's playing coy, I think, now she's goading me into action.

I get in the bath after her, me at one end and her at the other. As I hand her the bottle of champagne she grins. There's a glass waiting but she ignores it choosing to drink straight from the bottle and I watch with envy as a little trickles down her chin.

She passes it to me and I take a swig. But my eyes are on her, my attention is on her.

She smirks because she knows it.

I reach out and pull her right foot to me, slowly working my thumbs into the sole. She groans throwing her head back but she opens her legs as she does it, giving me the perfect view of her cunt through the water.

I reach for her left foot and as I work away the tension she uses her right to rub my cock. She's fixing me with a look too. She's ready, she's hungry. My angel needs to be fed again.

I thrust my hips forward letting her play with me for a bit as I grow harder and harder.

She drops a hand and starts touching herself as she does it and I watch entranced. The faces she's making, the way her mouth opens into an 'o' as she teases herself makes me want to film this and play it over and over.

Suddenly she's laying now with her legs spread, one over one edge and one over the other. Her knees are bent, her body is angled in a way that's begging me to fuck her. I push off from the side and she moves her other hand to grope her breasts. Fuck my woman knows exactly how to get what she wants. And right now we both know she wants me. My touch. My body. My cock in her.

"You're a demanding little thing aren't you?" I murmur.

She nods, thrusting her hips, rubbing against herself. The water laps around her cunt because I didn't have the patience to wait for the bath to fill completely.

"You called me a queen." She says. "Your queen."

I tilt my head waiting for whatever she's going to say next.

"And your queen needs your cock right now." She purrs.

Yeah she does. I grab her thighs, pinning her legs back further and slide into her. She lets out a low groan.

"Better your highness?" I say.

She nods. "This is where you belong now." She states as if she can command me and she's right. She can, she can tell me to do anything and I will. And second to that, her cunt is exactly where I belong, where I rule, where I master the world from.

She tries to move her hand away from her clit and I grab it.

"Touch yourself while I fuck you." I say.

Her face is flushed, her lips are a beautiful shade of pink right now and as I start thrusting into her I watch as she matches each move with a slow, deliberate circle of her clit.

"You like watching me." She says.

"You like me watching you." I reply.

She nods. I can feel her body clenching around my cock already and I love that this is turning her on as much as it is me. That her kinks are my kinks. That we have the same, twisted soul.

"My knight in shining armour." She murmurs and that gives me pause. Just for a second.

"I'm not your hero Eleri do you understand that?" I say as I begin sliding my dick in and out of her. I don't know why I need to get the words out but I do. I want her to understand what this is. Who I am because I'm not going to pretend, to lie, to lead her on with false pretences.

She moans in response shutting her eye.

"Look at me when I'm fucking you right now." I snap. In this moment I want her attention, I want every piece of her.

She obeys like the perfect creature that she is.

But as she stares at me with that almost innocent look I don't care what I was about to say. I don't care about anything. I lean down, kissing her hard. She grunts at the new, deeper angle of my cock in her but apart from that she doesn't complain. But then why would she? She loves my cock already. She's moulding around it as we speak.

"Fuck Nico." She gasps.

"When I cum you cum." I say.

She nods, biting her bottom lip, obviously trying to stave off the orgasm she's so desperately close to having.

"That's it, good girl." I say taking her face in my hands. She shudders again. I think if it wasn't so hot in here she would still have sweat on her brow from the concentration.

"Please…" She whimpers.

I pick up the pace, fucking her relentlessly now and a part of me doesn't care if it hurts. I need to cum. I need her to cum. We both need this and just as her walls constrict so tightly around me I think she might snap my dick in half, I let go, I fall, I claim my very own piece of heaven deep inside her as her screams ring in our ears.

She slumps back, her pussy already leaking out our juices as I slip from her.

She's breathing heavily, her chest is rising rapidly and I lay beside her watching her tits move.

For a moment I see a flash of her, not in that place they took her too, not forced to sit on one of their laps, but the first assault, the real insult, the one that left her broken in the alleyway.

"No one will ever hurt you again." I say quietly. Maybe it's more to myself than to her but the words need to be spoken all the same.

She turns her face to look at me. "And yet you claim not to be my hero." She half teases like she doesn't get what I meant.

I narrow my eyes. "I'm not Eleri. I'm not a hero. I'm not a good man. I've done things, bad things."

"Like earlier?" She says as if we both haven't technically committed murder today.

"Worse than that."

"Worse than killing someone?"

I give her a hard look but she doesn't flinch, she doesn't even blink, she just stares right back at me.

"I don't need a hero." She states. "And I certainly don't want one. So what exactly are you trying to tell me?"

"That I'm a selfish man. I take what I want. I do what I want. I don't care what anyone thinks. I don't give a fuck about anyone else. I won't shower you in roses, I won't..."

"Are you saying this like I have a choice? Like you gave me a choice?"

I smirk. She's right. I didn't. I didn't care if she wanted me, not at first because I knew eventually she wouldn't turn me down. I just didn't expect us to become this so soon.

"I will burn this world, rip it to pieces, annihilate everyone that gets in my way if I have to."

"Would you kill me?" She asks. Her voice is calm. She's making it sound like this is a normal conversation though I can see in her eye the seriousness behind her words.

For a moment I think of her, of the woman I loved before, of how she deceived me, of how she died. "If you ever betrayed me. If you..."

She places a finger across my lips to mute my words. "I won't. I will never do that but just so we're clear, if you ever betray me, I'll blow your fucking brains out."

My lips curl. I suck her finger into my mouth. For what should be a serious conversation she's already making my dick hard with the way she's just threatened me.

She lets me suck on it for a moment before she pulls it out with a popping sound.

"You are something else." I say.

"Says you." She replies as she slips her hand down, as she starts fondling me under the water. I groan. I'm semi-hard. I don't think I could fuck her again so soon but I'm not adverse to her trying.

She straddles me, rubs her tits in my face, lets me bury myself between them as she slowly brings my cock back up to attention.

"You keep this up and you might break it." I say.

"You've already torn me." She replies.

I raise an eyebrow. I thought I had. I couldn't see how else it would've ended, fucking her as I did without any lube.

"Not going to apologise for it?" She asks as her hand works its way so deliciously down to the base of my cock.

"Why should I? You liked it well enough." I say before groaning as she sinks herself on top of me again. Jesus this girl might be the death of me but what a way to go.

I smirk making a point of looking at where our bodies are now joined as if it proves my point.

"I like when it hurts." She says. "I like when you hurt me."

"Why?"

She shrugs. "I like the feel of it."

"What else do you like?"

"This." She says raising her hips, rolling them, moving that delicious fat ass of hers in such a way I can't help but grab hold of it. "I like having you like this." She half whispers as if it's a secret we don't already know. "Having such a man as you at my mercy."

"Who else has been at your mercy?" I ask feeling a streak of jealousy at the fact she's even insinuating she's been with someone else, though we're both more than aware the other wasn't a virgin when we met.

"No one that matters." She says.

I grab her throat tightly and she gasps but she rolls her hips too. She's still turned on, even in this moment. My aggression is a kink for her too it seems.

"No one else matters but me. Do you understand?" I state. She nods. "It's you. It's only ever you." She replies.

I release her throat, grab her waist, start thrusting up to meet her. "No one fucks you but me. You're mine Eleri. This cunt is mine. This body is mine. All of you is mine."

"Only yours." She says. Her tits bouncing as if they're nodding in agreement. "Yours to do what you want with. To use how you want."

I smile. Fuck my woman is perfect. So fucking perfect.

I take her right breast between my teeth, half yanking on it as it bite. Maybe I'm a mad man. Maybe I am everything the world says I am but in this moment I don't care. She's mine, all of her is mine and I'll fuck her how I want to.

She cries out, rocking her hips, fucking me back. "Make it hurt." She gasps. "I want your teeth marks as scars."

I grip harder, tear into her flesh and I can taste her blood when it splits. She's writhing in a mixture of pain and ecstasy and this time when we cum I don't even have to tell her to wait. She knows what I want, she knows what I need and she milks my cock so much I don't think I have anything left in my balls.

Her

CHAPTER
Twenty

I wake up in another strange bed. I think I must have gotten used to the size and the smell of Nico's because this one feels so alien. I roll over and he's there, beside me, awake, staring right back with those dark penetrating eyes of his.

"Hi." I say almost bashfully. As we haven't seen each other naked, as if I haven't begged him to fuck me so many times.

"Good morning." He says back with his low throaty voice that sends a shiver of something through me. God this man is a marvel. Why he picked me I don't think I'll ever know or truly understand but I don't care. I have him and that's all the matters.

I run my hand over his skin, feeling the lightness of his chest hair. He's so masculine. So full of testosterone. He's all alpha male and though I should be running from the hills with all the dangers this man presents I refuse to. I refuse to even consider it.

He pulls the cover back to reveal my breasts and then he runs his fingers over the livid bruising of where his teeth were. I wince slightly as he does it.

"Was I too rough?" He asks.

"No. I liked it." I reply glancing down, seeing where each individual tooth is ingrained in my flesh and seeing too where my skin has tiny scabs from where they punctured it.

He circles them, one nipple and then the other. I lay watching his face, staring at him as he does it. I can feel my nipples hardening for him, I can feel my pussy already throbbing and though I'm sore, really sore, I want him to fuck me right now all the same.

My hand finds his dick and of course he's hard. Morning wood and all that.

"I have work to do." He says.

"Then you'd better be quick." I reply and he raises an eyebrow.

"I'm not quick Eleri. Why should I be?"

I roll on top of him, straddle him, holding his dick and presenting it against myself, nudging at my entrance. I'm not taking no for an answer. He's the one that forced us to wait and now that I know how he feels inside me I'm not giving up any opportunity to have it again.

"Then I guess you'll be late." I murmur against his lips.

His eyes flash for a moment. I wonder if I've pushed too far and I feel a spike of adrenaline flood through me and I know he can tell.

He flips me, suddenly he's on top and his dick is pounding into me before I can think, before I can speak. The air is gone from my lungs. I'm half gasping with the force of him.

"My woman needs a good fucking again does she?" He says. One hand on the head board, one hand on my jaw.

I nod, I moan, I cry out at the mixture of pain and pleasure. I can feel every tiny tear inside me and without any lube he's doing it again despite how turned on I am. Despite how wet I am.

But I don't want him to stop. I'd rather he ripped me apart, tore me to pieces than stopped.

"You feel so good. Your tight little cunt loves my cock in it doesn't it?" He growls.

"I need it." I gasp. "I need you."

"Yes you do. My needy little whore."

I cry out again. It's louder this time and it echoes in the air. He feels so good. I shut my eye focusing on the feel of him, the way his cock slides in and out, the way my body practically moulds to him. I've never felt anything like it. I'll never want anything like it except from him. Only him.

"Fuck I'm going to cum." I gasp.

"That's a good girl. Cum for your king." He says as my body starts to lose control, as I start to thrash, and scream.

He roars as my muscles clamp down hard onto him and I think the feel of it sends him over the edge too because I can feel him pouring himself into me. His face is flushed, his eyes are shut as he lets his own orgasm take over.

And then he falls back onto the sheets, as if I've taken every bit of his energy. His body is sweaty, glistening and I want to roll my tongue along it and taste what I've done, what I've created.

But he has to get up. And I won't distract him further.

He clambers out of the bed, his dick swings between his legs as he walks through to the bathroom.

When he comes back out he's washed and dressed.

I get up, figuring I can shower once he's gone and he grabs a robe and hands it to me.

"You'd better put this on if you're coming downstairs." He says before heading out the room.

I frown before realising someone else is down there. No doubt waiting for Nico while we've been fucking.

I follow quickly after him. Maybe I am needy but I don't want him to go without saying goodbye. As I reach the main living space I see Preston sat now having a low conversation with Nico.

They both look at me and I blush. Like a silly little girl. I can't help it. I guess some part of me still can't get my head around all of this.

"I don't have anything to wear." I say realising all I've got are my dirty panties from yesterday and his suit jacket. I don't even have any shoes.

"I know." Nico replies. "I've arranged for clothes to be brought here. Some designers will be bringing their wares and you can pick whatever you want."

"I can pick?" I tease stepping closer to him. My last wardrobe was entirely of his choosing so I'm surprised he's giving me this autonomy.

"Just remember what I like to see you in." He says fingering the edge of my robe where it crosses over my breasts.

"I thought you preferred me without clothes?" I murmur and I see his lips twerk. I like amusing him. For some reason it makes me feel like we have more than just our physical attraction.

"Talking of which." He says pulling something from his pocket and handing it to me.

"What is it?" I ask.

"Birth control." He says fixing me with a very certain stare.

My eyebrow raises. I guess it makes sense. We haven't used protection so far and as fun as this is we are only just getting to know each other, the last thing we need is for me to fall pregnant.

I examine the packet. "It's only the morning after." I say feeling infinitely aware of the fact Preston is right here listening to every word.

"Preston is arranging for the doctor to prescribe something more long term." Nico says and I glance at him then, at his right hand man.

He meets my gaze but he doesn't seem embarrassed. He doesn't seem to have any sort of reaction whatsoever, as if all of this is perfectly normal. For a moment I wonder if they've done this before. Preston providing contraception for whoever Nico was fucking that month. I feel a stab of jealousy at the thought, and I feel a bit of anger too, that this might be all it is, me being flavour of the month.

Nico's arms have crept back around me. His hands are in their usual place, grabbing my ass, claiming my cheeks as his domain.

"I thought you were running late." I say to him.

"I am." He says. "You're very distracting."

I laugh. "I don't mean to be."

Preston snorts then and we both look at him.

"I'm going." Nico says letting me go. "You two play nice."

My eyebrow raises and I look between them.

"You get to spend the day with me princess." Preston says.

Nico throws him a look before kissing me and walking out.

"Why?" I ask as soon as he's gone.

"We thought it would be best, considering yesterday's turn of events."

"How is you being here best?"

"Eleri." He says, using my name for what I think is the first ever time. "You're not stupid. You're not some empty headed bimbo…."

"Thanks for clarifying that."

He gives me a look that says 'shut the fuck up for once'.

"…You know there's something going on. Nico wants to make sure you're safe. That you're protected. That nothing further happens to you."

"And what about him?" I say. "Who keeps Nico safe?"

"He's a big boy. He's more than capable of taking care of himself."

I shake my head. That's not a good answer in my opinion.

"You should wash." He says sounding like my parent. I roll my eyes and head upstairs. He's right I need to wash. I stink of sex. I can smell it oozing out of me, just like Nico's cum right now.

When I've showered I come back down wearing a different robe but a robe all the same. Preston looks at me as if I'm doing it on purpose. Flaunting myself.

"I have nothing to wear." I say.

He glances at his watch. "In little over an hour you will." He replies.

I sigh. "I want a coffee." I say as my stomach rumbles. "And maybe some food too."

"You should probably take this pill sooner rather than later." He says in a way that sounds like he wants to make sure I do.

I Ignore the underlying suggestion and simply nod as he slides it over the counter to me. He's right anyway, the sooner I take it the more effective it will be.

"How do you like your eggs?" I say picking up the phone.

"Excuse me?"

"I need food and I'm not going to eat alone." I say. "Nor am I going to have you watching me."

He laughs. We both know he's seen enough of me to date. In fact all of Nico's men have. But oddly someone watching me eat feels like a step to far, even though watching me fuck is okay? I shake my head at my absurd logic and try to ignore the growing arousal at the thought of Nico's dick. God he is right, I am a whore for him, and I don't think I want to change it.

When I'm done ordering and have taken the god damn tablet I sit opposite him, making a point of looking at him.

"What?" He says.

"Are you here to watch me?" I reply.

"I already said why I was here."

I sigh. "I'm not a little girl. I can take care of myself."

"I don't doubt that."

"Then why…"

"What did you do?" He asks cutting across me. "What exactly did you do to make him interested in you?"

I stare at him flabbergasted. "I don't know."

He snorts giving me a look that could almost be of derision. "I didn't do anything. I didn't want to be noticed. I didn't want to be seen. I was happy being invisible." I state.

"You chose to work at that bar though. What did you expect?"

"I didn't have a choice. Nowhere else would hire me with my face." I snap. He's acting like I planned this. Like I'm some conniving jezebel out to milk his boss for all he's got. Only he's got the wrong end of the stick because I'm not interested in Nico's material wealth, I'm not going to milk him of that but I'll more than happily milk his cock every day of the week.

"And now? Do you think you have a choice now?" He asks.

I shrug. "Nico is a man who's used to getting what he wants." I state.

"And right now he wants you."

I nod. I'm not denying that.

"Given the choice would you be here now? Would you chose to be with him?" He says.

I snarl. "What the fuck do you take me for? I'm not some common whore. I don't just let him fuck me because of who he is. I want him, just as much as he wants me."

He smirks as if he's proud to have pushed me so far, as if he's proud to have made me confess it. To admit that I'll let his boss fuck me for as long as he wants and when he eventually grows bored and no doubt casts me off for someone who has two eyes and a proper face I won't even begrudge him for it.

Though I'm ashamed to admit even to myself how much my heart would break when that happens. How much that rejection, that betrayal would hurt more than the acid did against my skin.

CHAPTER
Twenty-One

"Is this okay?" She says.

She's wearing a short, shimmery dress that clings to her curves with a neckline so low I know she's not wearing a bra. As she spins I see her nipples catch on the light. She feels sexy. She looks sexy. Everyone in the god damn club will be staring at her.

My cock throbs to life and I shift awkwardly in my seat. We don't have time for anything so for once I need to pretend that this woman isn't having the effect she is.

Her hair is styled, in big bouncy curls that if anything accentuate the big hourglass figure she has. She's done her makeup too. Nothing too heavy, nothing too much, just the perfect amount to make her perfect on my arm.

"You look beautiful." I tell her.

She pauses, tilting her head. I'm staring at her tits. I can't help it now. I'm half tempted to sack this whole evening off and just spend the next few hours with my face buried in her cleavage and my cock deep in her cunt.

"You won't be jealous, or angry?" She says.

"Of what?"

"Me going out like this. I can change. I can put something more covering on."

I smile. My woman is so considerate and yet so naïve at times. She thinks I would be jealous of other men, that I wouldn't want them to look at her, that I would somehow feel threatened by their glances?

"If this is what you want to wear then wear it." I say getting to my feet. My hands are on her waist, creeping up to cup her perfect fucking tits. "And they can look. I want them to look. Let them see what is mine."

She nods, her face flushing and I bet if I checked her panties would be wet with arousal.

I start circling her nipples, teasing them through the thin fabric. She lets out a moan and pushes into me more. I'm being a shit I know but I want her desperate for me tonight so when I eventually fuck her she cums harder than she has so far.

Because tonight one way or another, I'm going to make Eleri squirt.

A tap at the door breaks my game. She blinks but I see the disappointment in her face. She wants me to keep going. I drop my hold and take her hand.

"Come darling." I say leading her out and her ridiculous high heels click clack with every step.

We reach the club. My club. And the bouncers step back to let us in through the VIP entrance. Eleri is staring around us, wide eyed as if she's never been in a place like this.

The music is blaring, there's lasers and lights hitting all the surfaces. Bodies are dancing below us in the main crowd.

We walk into my personal area. It's like a great glass balcony over the theatre of what's below. I pull Eleri into the leather seat at my side. In truth I don't need her here, the first few hours will be boring, but I want her beside me, I want everyone else to see her face, to learn her name, to realise who she is.

And I want to give her a good time too. She's been cooped up in my house and then the hotel. It's not how I planned it, it's not how I would have played this out but it is what it is and so far she hasn't complained. She hasn't made a comment.

Blaine walks in and glances at her. I can see him running his eyes over her body and I tilt my head to challenge him. He grins back at me then clicks his fingers. The main doors open and in unison twelve men walk in.

The other twelve heads. Only they all answer to me. They take my direction. Their families exist, their families survive by my good grace.

They all tilt their heads, bow to me, and take their seats. Each exactly where I have designated.

Eleri glances at them but doesn't speak. She's so fucking perfect. She always knows when to ask and when to be silent.

I see a few of them glance at her. I see some of them stare at her face and I feel my anger flash. My hand reaches out and I'm touching her, pulling her to me for them all to witness.

"Allow me to introduce my queen." I say.

A few of them react. Most are wise enough to keep their faces neutral. It's a risky move to show Eleri off like this, to parade her. I've just put a target on her head, for my enemies she's now a person of significant interest. And yet I don't care. They won't touch her. They won't even get close.

But they will see this as a sign of weakness. They will think it's something they can exploit and that's exactly what I'm counting

147

on. I'm outmanoeuvring them. Out playing them. Lulling them into a false sense of security and when they think the chips are down I will make my moves.

We talk business for what feels like hours. I can see she's growing bored. I can see she's fidgeting despite her best efforts not to.

"Why don't you go dance?" I say in her ear.

"Without you?" She teases.

"I'll be along soon enough."

"Then I'll be down there, waiting." She murmurs before getting up in a way that gives me and me alone a perfect view of her tits.

I watch her go. Half the room watches her go. Her hips are swaying, her ass is mesmerising and I make a point of looking at every single one of them who is lusting after my woman right now. They gulp, caught red handed, but I don't say anything. I want them to look.

I want everyone to admire her, my beauty, my queen. Mine.

We talk some more. I sip my whiskey and listen more to the tone of what they're saying than their actual words. Most of them are with me. One or two are reluctant and I can see why, they are lesser families, they have more to lose, but as I point out, they also have more to gain from this.

"How do you know one of them isn't working for Emerson?" Preston says in my ear.

I grin. That's part of the plan. I'm counting on the very fact that at least one of them is. And anyway, there's only twelve men here. There should be thirteen. One of my disciples has already betrayed me. My judas has shown his hand by simply not turning up. Though I'm surprised it was him. Costas. I would have wagered his loyalty above some of the others in this room.

Talk turns mundane. There's girls in the room, some wives too. Blaine and few others discuss matters I'm not all that bothered with. Preston has some girl in his lap. My eyes flit down to the woman on the dancefloor staring up through the glass.

She's dancing, just like I told her to. Her body is undulating, swaying, moving in a rhythm that is hypnotic. Divine. I lean forward watching her more and I see a small smile creep onto her lips. She knows I'm watching her now.

It's as if it spurs her on, she dances more, she turns around and I watch as she grinds, as she manoeuvres that ass in a way I want to repeat with my cock.

Preston glances at where I'm looking and smirks. I think he's taken a shine to her. I think he's starting to like her too. And then his face changes, just a little.

I look back down and there's a man, he's touching her. She pushes him off and he tries again.

No doubt he's drunk but it's no excuse. Fucking entitled prick thinks he has a right to push it. A right to even look at her.

I'm on my feet. I'm done with this meeting anyway.

I storm down the stairs, push past onto the dance floor. It's still part of the VIP area so it's not as busy as the main arena.

Eleri spins around, she's looking at me, trying to articulate something over the loud music. I think she thinks she's angered me. That somehow that man taking liberties is her fault.

I grab her and my tongue is down her throat, silencing her words, claiming her. She moans against me and her tongue twists with mine as if she's desperate for me. I run my hands over her body, and she starts gyrating, dancing, giving me my own show. As she moves she grinds against me and I turn her round sticking my now throbbing dick against her ass.

She grinds harder. My filthy slut. My own personal little whore.

My hands slip under her dress and where her panties should be there's nothing, just a wet, needy slit.

I give her a questioning look and she bites her lip over her shoulder as if she knew this was how this evening would end. As if this was part of her plan.

She starts riding my fingers, covering them in her juices as she pleasures herself.

The club is dark, but not that dark. And anyway we're in the VIP area, there's only twenty or so bodies around us. Enough people can see what we're doing. And more are starting to notice.

"Does my queen need another seeing to?" I ask but I'm already unzipping my pants, pushing her up against the barrier.

"Yes." She moans. But of course she does. I've not fucked her nearly enough for her to be sated and after teasing her earlier I know she's been desperate for me.

"Fuck me Nico." She says.

"Oh I'm going to." I reply. "I'm going to fuck you so hard everyone here will know who your cunt belongs to." I half growl, making eyes with the man who dared to touch her who gulps but doesn't look away.

I lift up the back of her dress and position my cock. She tilts her hips encouragingly and uses her hands to brace herself. My little slut is so ready for me.

I slide into her and god is she wet.

I realise that she gets off on this too. On everyone seeing. On everyone witnessing.

I wrap my hand around her neck, I pull her body down at an angle. If she wants me to fuck her here then I'm going to do it my way. I'm going to show everyone in this club how I service her.

She's moaning louder and louder. My dick is pounding into her. Every time I bottom out she half yelps. I feel like I'm slamming into something inside that I shouldn't be but I don't care. She's not complaining. She's not telling me to stop.

My other hand sneaks around past her stomach and I pinch her clit. She shudders grinding more. Yeah she likes the pain, but I knew that already.

"My queen." I murmur in her ear as I fuck her and roll her clit at the same time I squeeze her neck.

She's losing it. Her legs are trembling. Her tits are half hanging out of the dress and I'm half tempted to rip if off her so that everyone can see the goddess that she is. That they can marvel at the beauty before them.

"Nico." She gasps.

I can feel her pulse racing under my hand. I know when I cum it's going to pour down her and she'll have to walk out with it there for everyone to see.

"Oh shit. Oh shit." She says and she's shaking more, jerking. She's cuming. My angel. My woman is cuming right here on the dancefloor.

I look up at the glass and half my men are watching too. I smirk.

My court is here, my queen is ready. I will coronate her here, right now, for everyone in this club to see. For this entire city to witness.

She cries out and it feels like her body flushes with something as she grips my cock so tightly. It pours down, over my dick, over my trousers, wetting us both.

My woman has squirted. Right here. My wanton angel has done exactly what I wanted her to. And before all these witnesses.

Fuck she really is perfect.

CHAPTER
Twenty-Two

It's pouring out of me. I don't even know what it is. It could be cum, it could be piss for all I know.

Nico is still fucking me. He's relentless.

I look around and everyone is watching, staring. How the hell have I not even noticed until now?

I should feel ashamed. I should feel humiliated but I'm not. I fucking love it.

I move my hand to join his. I want him to know how good this is for me, how much I want him to continue.

"You're so fucking perfect." He says in my ear and I turn my face to kiss him.

Our fingers are both circling my clit and then he pulls out. His dick is gone and suddenly he's ramming it into my ass.

I cry out. I've never even done anal before but to have it like this, with no lube and Nico's impossibly sized dick? It hurts. I can't lie, it really hurts but I don't care because it's Nico doing it. Him holding me down, fucking me in the ass for this entire damn club full of people to witness.

His hand moves on my clit again. I whimper because it feels so sensitive but he's such a fucking god he knows how to get me right back to my horny state within seconds.

He fucks my ass slower, more considerately. Maybe he can tell I've never done it before. Maybe he just wants this to be different.

I raise my hips, adjusting my stance because I can't take the angle I'm at. I think Nico takes it as encouragement though and he starts fucking me harder and I feel myself tear despite the newfound pleasure of it.

I cry out again and his fingers work to bring me back to another orgasm.

I shut my eye, I screw my face up as I scream a second time.

"Cum for me." Nico half orders in my ear but I barely hear it over the sound of the music and my own noise. All I can think is that he hasn't cum yet. He's still going. How the fuck is he still going?

And then he pulls out one final time, turning me to face him and cums all over my dress.

I gasp staring up at him and god help me he's grinning. This man of mine.

He runs his hands over it, spreading his cum through the fabric and onto my breasts.

"I love you." I say it before I even think not to. In this moment I really do. I fucking love this man.

He grins tweaking my nipples, making sure I'm totally covered in him. Marked for every one of these fuckers to see.

"I think I made my point." He says and I laugh. Yeah he did more than that.

As we go to walk off I realise half the people around us are stripping, fucking, touching themselves. It's like a god damn orgy in here now.

"Look what we started." I say.

"What you started." He replies.

"You were the one who fucked me."

He grins. "You were the one desperate for it."

"I wasn't desperate." I state.

"No?" He says turning to face me. "Do I need to remind you of how wet your cunt was?"

"Do I need to remind you that I'm covered in your cum right now?"

He steps up to me, his shirt almost touching me as he runs his hands back over me, focusing once again on my tits as I try so hard not to moan. He's just so fucking good.

"Desperate." He murmurs before stepping back and leading me out.

Him

CHAPTER
Twenty-Three

"They're ready for you."

I look up. Blaine is stood, arms crossed in the doorway to my office.

"That was quicker than I expected." I reply.

"What did you expect?" He says. "I like to overachieve."

Yeah he sure does. And he's certainly done it this time. Because I gave him a near impossible task, track down three men with no names, no descriptions, nothing.

And yet he did it. In less than half the time I mentally allocated to him.

"The photo helped." He says.

Yeah the photo helped. And I have Eleri to thank for that. I've spent the best part of two years trying to work out who the fuck they were and the day she lay that photo in front of me I at least got a piece of the puzzle.

If I'd been smarter I would have chased them down, would have got surveillance footage of them following her prior to the attack, but my focus was her and I wasn't as smart as I am now.

I pick up my phone. "Bring her." I say as Preston picks up.

He's the only one I'm leaving with her. Because of the bar I feel like she's more familiar with him, more comfortable too and he won't say or do stupid shit either.

I sit in the back of my car, flexing my hands, preparing myself for a moment I have waited so long for. When we reach the ruins Eleri is already there. Standing awkwardly beside Preston, looking confused, looking afraid too.

I walk up to her and she gives a small smile. She has no idea what's about to happen. No idea of the gift I'm about to bestow on her.

"What is this?" She says looking around.

"You'll see." I say taking her hand and leading her through the murky remains of what was once a graveyard.

I guess it should be unnerving. That's why we picked this place. A disused, bombed out wreck of what was once a majestic church. The only part that remains is under the ground.

And the fear factor of bringing your enemies here, half dragging them into the dark is what makes this place so resplendent.

She's wearing a white dress, I couldn't have picked it better because she looks more like an angel right now and the symbolism doesn't escape me. That she's here, in this place of sin, in this place of death, like a virginal sacrifice.

And a part of her will be sacrificed tonight. A part of her will be gone. Because tonight, together we will strip away the last vestiges of her innocence. She will embrace the dark, she will relish herself in it. Even if I have to drag her the entire way.

She will be reborn in the blood of the men who tried to ruin her.

I step down the stone stairs first. She stays in my shadow as if it might provide protection.

As soon as we reach the bottom we hear it. We feel it too. The water trickling from above. The sound of our shoes with each step we take and most of all the four men's fear as they huddle, on their knees waiting.

There are only a handful of men here beside us. Two are on the doorway, both armed to ensure our playthings are obedient. The others hang back.

None of my men like coming here. No one except Blaine, though even he understands that this moment is for me and Eleri alone.

"Who are they?" She asks.

"Don't you remember them?" I say turning to watch her because I want to pinpoint the exact moment when she realises what's happening.

She frowns stepping nearer. One of the men in the middle mutters something incomprehensible and she turns her face to focus on him.

"They're…" She trails off turning to look at me. "They're…"

"Yes." I say. "They're a gift for you."

Her face flits from surprise to fury. And god is she beautiful to behold. She spins back around. All her fear, all her trepidation is gone now. My queen has come to life.

"What are you going to do with them?" She asks. She's pacing around them now. Her confidence has grown so much in the last few seconds.

"What do you want to do?" I ask her back. It's a test though she doesn't know it. If she says spare them I know we've got more work to do. That this night will be hard on her, hard on her soul. I won't of course. I kill them all just the same. But if she says what

159

I hope she will then I know she really has embraced the part of herself that I hunger to see.

She fixes her eye on them. Each of them one by one before looking at me.

"I asked you to kill him." She says pointing to the man who muttered, the man from the tattered photo she presented. "I said I wanted him dead."

"Do you still want me to kill him?"

She shakes her head and my heart deflates just a little. I thought after she killed that guy who was trying to rape her, I thought after everything I've tried to tease out of her so far that we were getting somewhere. That she was becoming who she's meant to be. Embracing the dark.

"I want to." She says.

"What?"

"I want to do it. They attacked me. They beat me. Tried to violate me. They stole half my sight." She finishes in a snarl and even I feel the anger raging through her blood right now. "I deserve to take their lives. I deserve at least that much."

"Yes you do." I say smiling.

She takes a sharp intake of air and her eye falls on the table to her right. She then looks at me as if for permission. Only this is her court. She is the judge, jury, and executioner here.

Whatever justice she decides it will be delivered by her hand. I'm just here to bear witness to it.

She picks up a knife. It glints in the dingy light and all four of them mumble like the pathetic, useless waste of oxygen that they are.

"Shall we begin?" She says and then I watch as my magnificent queen delivers the justice she has waited so long for.

She cuts, she gouges. The men scream. It's a marvel to watch. A feast for my eyes. Blood flies everywhere. It splatters the wall, it covers her dress. She becomes a piece of art, the finest painting the world has seen. Her face, her scar, her skin is drenched in it but she doesn't stop, she doesn't even wipe any of it off, she merely lets it drip down and I stare at her beautiful body, marvel at her hardened nipples under all the coppery redness.

One of them tries to escape. He crawls on his bound hands and I put my foot on his back to hold him.

Eleri looks over with something like amusement in her face.

"Remember how I crawled?" She says walking slowly to him. "Remember how I cried? How I begged? How I pleaded?"

He whimpers. It's pathetic to hear but incredible to watch. She crouches down, the knife is in her left hand and she stabs it into his back. Drives it between his flesh.

She then rises, takes another knife, a clean one, and continues her performance.

By the time she is done three of the four men are dead. Carved up, butchered. She sliced their dicks off. She cut great strips into their limbs and when their blood was pouring like a river she took her time carving each of their hearts out of their chests.

The last man is still beneath my boot. He hasn't moved though we both know he's alive from all the whimpering he's making.

She walks up to me but her focus is on the man at our feet. She squats down, grabs his head by his hair and yanks it back as he half yelps. I'm surprised he has the energy left to make any sound but I'm pleased he does. His cries, his fear is delectable.

In one smooth, almost practiced motion Eleri slides the blade along his throat, slicing it right open. He gurgles, he splutters, his blood sprays out and she tosses the blade before running her hands through it.

She grins at me licking the taste of it from her fingers and then her mouth is against mine and I can taste it too. Taste the rusty iron on her tongue.

My avenging angel. My perfect fucking queen.

CHAPTER
Twenty-Four

We're in the bath. Again.

We had to shower when we got back. Shower off all the blood and all the dirt too.

And now I'm lying against him, listening to his breathing, relishing the fact that he gave me that moment. He allowed me to do whatever I needed. He let me vanquish my demons without intruding, without feeling like he needed to be a part of it.

"What are you thinking?" He says.

"Thank you."

"For what?"

"For giving me that."

He kisses the side of my head. The side with the scar. The side where I should be able to look at him but I can't. Somehow I don't mind it so much now.

"How did you know?" I ask.

"About what?"

"The other men."

"Blaine found the first. He roughed him up a bit till he told us who the others were."

"But you knew before. You said it before. You said there were others before even I did."

He narrows his eyes. "Do you want the truth?"

"Yes."

He shifts, moving around so that he's no longer behind me but sat across, facing me. As if I need space now to hear whatever it is he's going to say.

"I was there." He states.

I frown. "Where?"

"That night."

I blink. I think my heart stops for a second. What the fuck is he saying right now?

"I saw you in that bar. I watched your performance. I was going to approach you after. You were mesmerising...."

I'm staring at him. I know I am. How the hell was he there? How the hell am I only just hearing this? And then my mind registers something else, that he saw my face, he saw how I was, how I used to look. I feel my heart clench at that. He knew me before. He knew what I looked like.

"...I saw you go outside for a cigarette. I saw you reject that man through the window."

I gulp. I haven't had a cigarette since. I haven't sung since either. That's partly why I ended up working in Nico's bar. Because I have no other skills. I have no qualifications. I was a singer. That was my life. And they stole that from me the night they stole my face.

"Did you see them? When they attacked me?" I ask. My voice sound so cold now. So harsh.

He winces. "I heard your screams. I didn't realise they had followed you. I didn't realise what they were planning."

"They wanted me to fuck them." I say. Not that it wasn't obvious.

"I know."

"They waited for me. They waited outside the bar. They followed me, assaulted me. I ran but I wasn't fast enough."

"It's not your fault." He states.

I pull a face. That's not what they said. Not what they shouted when they poured that acid over me.

"Eleri…"

I shake my head. I don't want to hear it. That night ruined a part of my life but I'm done obsessing over it. Done letting one awful moment dictate everything else.

"Do you want to hear the rest?" He asks.

"What do you mean?"

"There's more." He states.

"What?"

"There's no such thing as the City Ward Memorial Fund." He says so calmly I think I must have misheard him.

"Excuse me?" What the fuck is he saying. That fund paid for my medical bills. That fund literally saved my life.

"It was a front. It was my money. All of it."

I'm shaking my head. I think I'm trembling too. I can see the water rippling around me.

"I did it for you. Everything since your attack, every part of your life has been planned by me." He states.

"Why?"

"Why do you think?"

It can't be. This man is mad. He has to be mad.

"I made sure no one else would employ you. I wanted to keep you close. Under my watch if you will. I had my men follow you each night you walked home to make sure no one could hurt you. Even your apartment was of my choosing."

"Why?"

"Because you are mine Eleri. From that night I first laid eyes on you, you have always been mine."

"But I'm ruined. Look at my face. I'm a monster."

He grins. "No you are not. You're the most beautiful creature I've ever seen." He pulls me to him and a part of me thinks I should resist but I don't. I just let him hold me to his chest, let him stroke my hair, listen to the beating of his heart for so long I think I might have turned into a statue.

"I've never had anyone." I say quietly. "I was used to being on my own."

"What about your family?"

I pull a face. "My family? My father died when I was sixteen. He was a drunk and he fell into the river and drowned. And my mother married another man not long after. He was a drunk too. He would hit her. Hit me as well when he thought he could get away with it. I ran away. I left and came here."

"And got a job as a singer?"

I nod. "I was doing great. I'd been here for six years. I was happy. My life was good. And then that night happened and everything changed."

"It shouldn't have ended like that. It wasn't supposed to. You should have come home with me." He says so confidently I let out a laugh.

He kisses my shoulder. "But you're here now. And I'll never let you go."

"What are you saying?" I ask looking at him.

"You are my queen Eleri. You always have been. And no matter what happens, I will always be proud to have you at my side."

"Then let me help you."

"With what?"

"Whatever the hell is going on. I know something's happening. Those men that raided your house tells me something is going down. Preston even told me so."

He narrows his eyes. "It would be dangerous."

"I'm not afraid of getting hurt."

"I know that but my instincts are to protect you."

"As are mine for you." I snap back.

He smirks. His hands are on my clit before I realise it and I'm spreading legs even though I know it's a distraction.

"My little fighter." He says. "My own personal warrior."

I nod, rocking my hips, welcoming his touch more. He grabs my ass, holding me up and thrusts his cock into me before holding me still against his chest as if he wants me to simply keep it warm.

"Let me help." I gasp. He's so fucking big that just having him in my pussy is enough to make me feel things.

He starts thrusting, slow, deliberate movements and each one makes me see stars.

"Please." I half beg.

"Please make you cum or let you help?" He teases.

"Both." I say digging my hands into his thighs riding his cock, letting my ass cheeks slam against him.

He leans forward, wrapping his hand around my throat, just like he did back at the club and god do I love it. His other hand is already claiming ownership of my clit and he's starting to pound into me harder and harder.

"You really want to help me?"

"Yes." I gasp both in encouragement and in answer to him. Only it's so hard to focus, so hard to even think.

"You're sure? I may ask you to do things you don't want to."

"I'd do anything for you." I half shout. The intensity, the feel of his cock is too much. But I don't want to cum yet. I want to hold off till he says the words. Till he grants me my wish.

"Anything?" He questions.

"I'd kill for you Nico."

He grips my throat harder, my breath catches and I let myself go. I let myself cum as he pounds into me over and over and over. "Good girl. Clench around my cock." He groans as he cums too. "Clench hard and milk me good."

We lay back in the water both panting. His cock is still in me and I refuse to move, refuse to let him go.

"You'll have to do everything I say. Exactly as I say." He states.

"I already do." I murmur. It's true. I'm so obedient he could tell me to jump off a cliff and I would. He could tell me to climb to the tallest tower in this city and fuck myself for everyone to see and I'd do it happily knowing it was what he wanted.

What he needs of me.

Him

CHAPTER
Twenty-Five

We're sat around the table. Me, Preston to my left, Blaine to my right. Behind us are at least a dozen of my men. Though they're not armed, the fact that they're there is a warning enough.

Opposite us is Emerson Dalconti. With the biggest smirk on his face that I'm itching to wipe off.

"This doesn't have to be any messier than it already is." The man beside him says. He's a cousin of Emerson, Jace is his name. He's as much of an idiot as Emerson is if he thinks he can play games with me and live to tell the tale.

"Bit late for that isn't it?" Blaine says leaning forward, and they try not to look at the knife he's currently twisting around the palm of his hand and the blood that's dripping as a result. Yeah the man is a psycho but by god is he good getting under peoples skin.

"You started it by beating up the La Cruso boy." Emerson growls.

"Maybe you shouldn't send a boy to do a man's job." I state. Besides we both know Emerson was making moves before that. He wouldn't be stupid enough to lay his cards on the table without feeling like he had a few aces up his sleeves already.

Emerson stretches his hands as if he's imagining wrapping them around my neck and I half want him to do it, to cross the line, to step over the agreed safe zone so I can gut him and get it over with.

"These are our terms." He says. "You give up control of the docks to us. You agree to turn a blind eye to our trade and we'll do the same for you. Call it a union. A coming together of like-minded individuals."

I shake my head. We're not like minded. We might be in a similar line of business but I won't lower myself to the level they do. And I sure as hell won't allow such shit to operate right under my nose, unchecked, uncontrolled either. Besides I don't need a union. I run this city, and I sure as hell haven't fallen so low as to need to work with the Dalcontis.

"It's just a few girls." Jace says. "Why do you have such a problem with it?"

"A few girls?" Preston spits. He's as sickened by it as me.

"Apparently Nico Morelli has morals." Emerson says and the men behind him laugh.

"I don't trade children and I don't use children to make profits." I growl. I don't have an issue with prostitution per se. If a woman or a man for that matter wants to sell themselves go right ahead, my issue is when they're barely old enough to wear a bra and they've been trafficked in from god knows where with no control over what they do and who they fuck. That's where I draw my line.

"Say what you want Morelli because soon enough you'll be off the board, out of the game entirely." Jace says and Blaine lets out a laugh beside me.

"You wanna bet little boy?" He says getting up, stepping closer to the white chalk dividing the ground between us. I know he won't step, I know he's better than that but I like how they respond, how their whole bodies change when my man gets near.

"Tell your guard dog to step down." Emerson says.

"Tell him yourself. You've been so vocal so far." I reply.

He narrows his eyes, looking from me to Blaine. "Sit the fuck down." He says.

Blaine grins, giving them a perfect view of his solid gold teeth.

"I prefer to stand if it's all the same boys." He says and Preston lets out a laugh beside me.

"I can't wait for your kingdom to come crashing down." Jace says getting to his feet.

"You're so certain it will?" I say clicking my fingers, letting them see another roll of the dice. There's not a chance in hell of it. I'm out playing them even now.

Two of my men move behind us, dragging the beaten body of Enzo, Emerson's younger brother. He's been snooping around, fucking one of the girls from the bar for months, doing everything he can to get information.

He groans slightly as they toss his body right on the chalk.

"The fuck?" Emerson growls jumping to his feet.

"You think I didn't know what you were up to?" I say. "You think it wasn't obvious?"

Jace and Emerson exchange a telling look before they grab Enzo and drag him to their side.

"You'll pay for that Morelli." Jace says pointing his finger.

I laugh. "Sure I will." I state. Like this man has the balls to do anything, like he has the power to dethrone me.

173

"The fuck have you done to him?" Emerson says pulling his clothes back, seeing all the blood, despite the sutures.

"I'm just letting you know that your actions have consequences." I state. "Enzo here thought he could use his dick to your advantage, stick it where it doesn't belong and fuck with my business. Well he won't make that mistake again."

Blaine laughs. He knows what I'm getting at because he was the one who did it, who cut the man's dick right off. Though in truth it was Eleri that had given me the inspiration. Not that she knows it.

Enzo splutters, half choking and his dick rolls out of his mouth flopping on the floor. I look at Blaine. He shoved his dick in his own mouth?

Blaine grins at me. Of course he fucking did.

"You..." Jace begins taking a step towards us. Fists clenched like he's ready to start laying down punches.

"Not so fast little boy." Blaine says, pulling himself up. He's just one step away now, one step from initiating this.

Emerson grabs Jace yanking him back. "He needs a doctor." He says as if that justifies their cowardice.

"Better see to him then." I say.

Emerson glares at me but there's nothing else he can do in this moment but just retreat.

We sit, me and Preston and watch as they carry Enzo away and disappear with their tails between their legs.

Blaine stands the whole time, waiting for them, no doubt hoping they'll change their minds and he can get down to some real bloodletting.

When they're gone, when it's just us left he slinks back to his chair and growls with frustration.

I look over at Preston who's pulling a face.

"Don't tell me that wasn't necessary." I say.

"You cut his dick off." He says and both me and Blaine laugh.

"What else did you expect me to do?" I reply.

Preston sighs. Sometimes I wonder if he even understands me but then I see he's laughing. Blaine joins in and then all three of us are laughing.

"Did you see his fucking face?" Blaine says. "When his dick rolled out, did you see Emerson's face?"

I laugh louder. By the time I'm finished they'll all be in a similar state to Enzo, castrated, emasculated, their bodies showing on the outside what they are on the inside, worthless pathetic excuses for men.

Preston slides his phone to me. "We picked this up. Thought you should be aware."

I narrow my eyes, taking the screen, staring at the footage. "Where is this?" I ask.

"Few miles west of the city." He replies.

"You think he's actually back?" I ask.

He shrugs. "Looks that way."

I clench my fists. I know he's behind it, behind it all, all three of us know that but the fact he's got the balls to come out of hiding makes me realise he's grown up, evolved. He's not the same man I faced off against six years ago.

"I want you on this." I say to Blaine.

"I already am boss." He replies. But of course he is. That's why I have him. He already knows what I want, what I need before even I know it sometimes.

Him

CHAPTER

Twenty-Six

I'm out shopping. There's a big charity gala Nico is hosting this evening with anyone who's anyone invited.

And he wants me there.

Beside him.

As his date.

I guess I shouldn't be so shocked because from the offset he's made it clear he wants everyone to know I'm his. As if he's not ashamed of me. As if I'm someone worthy to be with such a man.

A smile creeps on my face at the thought.

That I'm there, in front of the entire city and all they can do is treat me with respect because Nico is making them. I never thought this was possible, that after the attack, after my face was ruined, that I'd ever live a normal life again, that I'd ever dare to raise my head and be noticed by anyone.

I flit from boutique to boutique. I have enough dresses already but I want to wear something daring. Something that shows off my body the way Nico likes.

He's giving me my own bodyguards. They follow behind me, making no comment as we go. I have a chauffeur too. It's surreal. I feel like a celebrity, a queen.

Once I find a dress that fits exactly what I want I decide to pop into a lingerie store. I want to surprise Nico with a few items as a treat. My bodyguards again don't comment but they stand at the door, looking slightly awkward amongst all the lace and frills.

I pick up a few items, a cut out set, a corset, some crotchless panties, all things I think Nico will appreciate me covering my body in.

"Miss Gordon?" A man says quietly as I'm holding a teal bra and trying to figure out if the colour would be draining or not against my skin tone.

I frown looking at him and then at my guards. I don't think they've seen him, we're pretty well hidden but I know I only have to call and they'll come running.

"Who are you?" I ask.

He flashes a badge. Subtly. Enough for me to see briefly and understand he's a cop.

"You've got yourself tangled up into a lot of mess." He murmurs. The authority dripping from his voice.

"I think you're mistaken there." I reply coolly.

"You're sleeping with Nico Morelli." He states like it's a secret. Like it's not his men standing at the door.

"What do you want?"

"Your boyfriend is not a good man. He runs the mob. He's killed a lot of people. Murdered them."

"Can you prove that?" I ask.

He smirks. "He's facing RICO charges that would mean he spends the rest of his life in jail. He and everyone associated with him." He pauses for dramatic effect. "How do you think you'd fare in the system? A woman like you?"

I screw my face up at him. He thinks he can persuade me to snitch of Nico is that it? Not a chance.

"We know he's controlling you, we know you're not fully complicit in this relationship despite your attempts to be…" He glances at the bra in my hand as if it's evidence of Nico's power over me. "Would you really throw your entire life away for such a man? If you work with us, give us information then I can help you avoid all that. You could have a new life, a new start. Without Nico Morelli controlling you."

I scoff. "He doesn't control me. I'm with him by choice. And you have nothing on him. Nico is a good man."

"His victims would disagree with you there." He states before making a point of studying my scar. As if he has a right too. "I'd have thought with your history you'd be more on the side of justice."

I scowl. "How dare you." I snap. "You have no idea what you're even talking about. Nico gave me more justice than you lot ever did. I'm loyal to him. I'll never betray him, even if he was the devil himself I would stand by his side and nothing you say would change that."

My bodyguards are suddenly here. Grabbing this piece of garbage and hauling him out before he can reply and tossing him into the street.

I take a deep breath, calming myself and go pay for the items I'm holding before gratefully getting into the waiting car.

I try not to think of that man. Of what he said. But I make a mental note to tell Nico. He needs to know that they're looking into him, investigating him. I need to warn him.

I spend the afternoon getting ready. I've arranged for someone to do my hair, to do my makeup too. I want to look perfect for Nico.

I want him to be proud of me.

He comes back to the hotel later than I expected but I know with whatever the hell is going on he's busy. Really busy.

He showers and gets in his tuxedo and sits, glass of whiskey in hand watching as I descend the stairs.

"What do you think?" I ask but I can already tell from the look on his face that he likes what he sees. He always seems to like what he sees.

The dress is an off the shoulder, fit and flare with a split up the side the whole way to the top of my thigh. I'm wearing a corset because a bra just wouldn't hold me and the fabric clings to my figure as if it's worshipping it. With my hair curled and tousled over the damaged part of my face I feel a million dollars right now.

"Perfect except for one thing." He replies pulling out a box and handing it to me.

I frown as I open it and my jaw drops. It's a necklace, a gold necklace with the biggest pear shaped diamond pendant I've ever seen.

"It's forty carats." He says as he takes it and unhooks the chain before sweeping my hair aside to fasten it around my neck.

The diamond nestles just above my cleavage and he smiles as he stares at it.

"This is too much." I half stammer.

"No it's not. And it's the first of many. I want you covered in diamonds. Covered in jewels."

I gulp. How the hell will I ever be able to show my gratitude to this man?

"Are you ready?" He asks bringing me out of my thoughts.

"I'm always ready for you." I say and he laughs.

CHAPTER
Twenty-Seven

We pull up outside the hotel. Paparazzi and photographers are everywhere. I can tell Eleri is nervous but when I look across at her she gives me a smile that's so full of confidence I swear my cock jerks.

I get out first and she exits gracefully, taking my arm, letting me guide her. All around cameras are flashing but she doesn't seem fazed. She just keeps her focus on me.

We walk the red carpet side by side.

I pull her to a stop at the very top of the stairs and she pauses, one leg outstretched through the split, her beautiful flesh on display and the cameras go wild snapping away at us. Snapping away at their king and queen.

And then we walk inside.

The place is already packed. The governor, politicians, even a few of Hollywood's finest are here. But we're the centre of attention.

Everyone's focus is on us.

Eleri is the perfect date. She speaks when addressed but most of the time she stays quiet preferring to talk more to me and me alone. As if her words are only for my hearing. As if her voice is only for me too.

We take our table. I make sure to see she has a glass of champagne and we sit as the compare welcomes everyone.

And then I get up and make my speech. It's short, to the point. Making clear that this is for charity. And they're all here by virtue of my good grace. I won't have them forget who feeds them, who provides their livelihoods.

When I sit back down there's an auction. It's tedious but necessary. I've thrown in a few items to look generous; a few paintings, some jewellery, they all sell and the proceeds will help build the illusion that I'm a philanthropist and not something more sinister.

When the bidding is done we get up. A band has started, people are dancing. I glance at Eleri and wonder whether to show off some moves while we're here. Of course our dancing will have to be a little more highbrow than back at the club.

Preston walks up to us and murmurs something about the Governor wanting a word. I grunt in reply. Of course he wants a word, he's running for office again and if the polls are anything to be believed he needs all the help he can get.

Eleri doesn't react when I state this. It's as if she understands now how much power I truly have. I wonder if I would have been more or less enthused with her if she was scared of me? Scared of how dangerous I am, of how much this entire world dances to my tune.

There's a small scuffle, a drunken man falls over and a few of my men move quickly to escort him out. Eleri glances around nervously as if she's on edge.

"Relax darling. My men are here." I murmur to here and point out where Blaine and a few others are stood ensuring this night goes exactly as I planned and that there are no, how do I put it, incidences.

"Nico…" She says quietly and I look at her, more because of the tone of her voice than anything.

"What is it?"

"That man, over there…" She pauses turning her back so if the man she's indicating looks he won't be able to see her face. "He's a cop."

"What?" I say looking to where Lucas is stood talking to Blaine. "He's not a cop Eleri." I say dismissively.

She grabs my arm, squeezing it. "No he is. He stopped me when I was out earlier. He told me they were investigating you. He said they have enough to put you away for a long time."

I narrow my eyes but she's not done yet.

"He tried to offer me a deal, if I talked…" She states.

I look at Preston who's standing awkwardly.

"What the fuck is this?" I snarl.

"It was Blaine's idea." He says.

"What was?" Eleri asks screwing her face, her expression going from concern to confusion.

"Why don't you get a drink? You're out of champagne." Preston says to her and she scowls but looks at me anyway.

"Go Eleri." I state. She nods obediently and walks away. Even now, even in this moment she's so perfectly queen like, trusting me, trusting my decisions because she knows I've got her back.

I wait only until she's far enough out of earshot.

"What the fuck is going on?"

"Blaine was suspicious. He thought she might be a mole." Preston says. "I told him it wasn't a good idea but he decided to go with it anyway."

"So what, Lucas pretends to be a cop, tries to see if she'll snitch, is that it?" I ask.

"If it makes you feel better she told him where to shove it." Preston replies.

"Of course she did." I say but I'm already crossing the room heading for Blaine.

He sees me coming as does Lucas.

"What the fuck is this I hear about you pretending to be a cop?" I growl.

Lucas squirms but Blaine doesn't.

"We had to be sure." Blaine says.

"Like fuck you did. She's my woman, do you think I'd be stupid enough not to vet her?"

"She appeared out of nowhere, what did you expect? And with everything going off with Emerson..." Lucas says.

I'm half tempted to punch him, to shatter his god damn face right here and be done with it.

"Eleri is not a spy." I state.

"Yeah?" Blaine says stepping nearer, only his eyes are darting behind me. "So how come she's talking to your brother right now?"

CHAPTER
Twenty-Eight

I don't know what's going on but it's clear some shit is happening. That someone is playing games. That his men think it's okay to test me.

I do my best not to storm over to the bar, not to scowl, to keep my face neutral and look like nothing's going on because this is Nico's night and I won't do anything to fuck with it despite how much I want to punch Blaine's stupid face right now.

I order a shot of vodka. No, it's not ladylike but no I don't care. I need something stronger than champagne, something with less bubbles too. I knock it back before ordering a second.

"Now why would such a delectable creature as yourself be sat drinking alone?" Someone says just as I feel fingers creeping down my back.

I turn glaring at the person who dared to touch me and his whole face reacts as he takes mine in. I guess I should be used to it now. Used to the shock, used to the horror, the revulsion in people's eyes when they see the scar, when they see the fact almost half my face is ravaged.

Before I can reply I feel Nico's hand, gripping me possessively and I feel like I'm suddenly caught between the two of them. Caught in a situation I don't understand.

"Hello Nico." The man's eyes flash as he leans back against the bar clearly assessing us both.

"Why are you here?" Nico growls.

He smirks. "You know I'm a soft touch when it comes to charity. Though apparently so are you it seems." He says looking at me before reaching out to run his fingertips down my shoulder.

Nico pulls me back, pulls me right off the stool and behind him so this man can no longer get close enough to touch me. And to say I'm grateful is an understatement.

"I meant what the fuck are you doing in this city?" Nico snaps.

Maybe I'm imaging it but he looks like Nico, just a little. The same face shape, the same jaw line and crevice in his chin. Even the ring on his little finger has the same crest as Nico's.

He sighs before taking a languid sip of his drink. Whiskey neat.

"I thought it was about time we had a proper conversation." He murmurs.

"You mean you're done having a paddy and are ready to act like a man for a change?"

He looks at me again. I want to snap at him, to ask what the hell he's gawping at but I hold my tongue. Something tells me Nico would prefer to handle this without my involvement.

"The family are meeting." The man replies swirling the amber liquid as he speaks.

"I decide when we meet."

He sneers stepping closer. "I think you're still labouring under the illusion that everyone follows your orders."

Nico grabs his shirt right at the collar where his bowtie hangs undone. "I think you're labouring under the misapprehension that I won't gut you right here…"

He laughs, dropping his grip from the glass and it splashes a little. "Calm down brother. You wouldn't want to look bad now, not in front of all these people…"

Nico snarls glancing round and we realise there are people already looking our way.

"I don't give a fuck what they think." Nico says.

"No? What about your little bambino here? You don't care what she thinks? Or is it just her cunt you care about because it's not like her face is anything to look at."

Nico goes to punch him and he laughs, moving his arm to reveal the gun under his jacket.

"Give me a reason." He taunts.

"You're not man enough."

"Maybe not, but by the time this is over one of us will be dead and it won't be me."

Nico laughs. "Sure thing Roman. Tell yourself that as lullaby if it helps you sleep at night."

He lets him go and Roman takes a moment to straighten his tux.

"It was nice meeting you sweetheart. I'm sure we'll see each other again soon." He says before turning and walking away.

Nico clenches his fist obviously weighing up the merit of going after him.

"Nico." I say quietly.

"What did he say to you?" He asks turning back to focus all his attention on me.

"Nothing. Just some cheap chat up line about me drinking alone and then he saw my face." I say trying not to wince. I shouldn't care what he thinks, what anyone thinks except Nico and yet it's hard to remember that when someone literally stands in front of you stating what a hideous creature you are.

He raises an eyebrow.

"Who is he?" I ask.

"My brother. My younger brother." He murmurs.

"I…" I fall silent at the look on his face. I didn't even know he had a brother. He's not mentioned his family once. Not even after I spoke about mine.

He lets out a low exhale of air. "Would you like to dance?" He says.

"Excuse me?"

"This is a charity event, I wanted to show you off…" He states taking my hand.

"I thought after that you might want to leave."

"Why would I do that?" He asks.

"You like to plan Nico. That's your style."

He smirks. "Maybe I do but right now I want to dance with you." He says leading me onto the dance floor and I feel more eyes on us.

"Can you actually dance?" I ask thinking of the last time we attempted to and how that ended up. I'm not sure how the city elite would feel if he decided to get his admittedly divine cock out and start fucking me here for them all to watch.

"Of course I can." He says before spinning me round so fast my breath catches in my throat.

"Is this your attempt at sweeping me off my feet?" I tease.

He laughs. "I thought I already did that?" He murmurs.

"What about Blaine and that other guy?" I ask. "Was he really a cop?"

His face remains passive but I see the anger in his eyes. "No he wasn't."

"So what that was a test? Of me?"

He doesn't reply. He doesn't need too. We both know what it was.

I grab his collar, meeting him head on. "I told you I'd do anything for you Nico. That wasn't a lie."

"I didn't think it was." He states.

Neither of us are dancing. We're standing still in the middle of the room while couples spin and turn around us.

"I meant what I said. I will kill for you."

"I know Eleri."

"Then tell your men that if they ever pull a stunt like that again they'll have to answer to me."

He grins for a moment before his mouth crashes into mine. I groan against him, letting him win for a second before I pull myself away.

"You make my cock so hard when you're like this." He says.

"Like what?"

"Fierce, fiery. My woman." He states.

I scoff. I'm not trying to turn him on right now, I'm trying to make a point.

"Do you always think with your dick?" I ask.

"When it comes to you Eleri, it's hard not to." He says. His hands are gripping my waist in a way that's almost indecent. I know if I look his dick will be there, erect in his pants, straining the fabric to get out.

"It looks like you need a little assistance?" I say glancing down, seeing that I'm right.

"Not a little." He says. "But I am done here."

"Meaning?"

"Meaning I'm taking you back to the hotel and fucking your brains out." He says taking my hand and leading me off the dance floor as I do my best to keep my own need under control.

Him

CHAPTER
Twenty-Nine

He had the audacity to be there. To show his face.

It's a power play. I know and he knows it.

And now he's called the family together. To meet. As if he's the head. As if he's in charge.

But what he doesn't realise is that this meeting he's calling is going to take an unexpected turn.

Preston is going over the finer details. He's drawn up a whole plan of the house. The Parthenon as we call it because my grandfather had a thing for ancient history and the façade has so many pillars it rivals the Greek temple itself.

But our gathering won't be in the main house. It'll be beneath it. In the cave-like basement constructed when my family needed more secrecy, more privacy than it does now. When it didn't hold as much power, when the other houses rivalled ours and we feared the sound of someone smashing our door in in the middle of the night and murdering our children as we watched.

But that was decades ago. My father built our empire and when I took over I built it even stronger.

And now my little brother thinks he can waltz right in and take it out from under me. He's a fool. An idiot. And he doesn't learn from his mistakes, which if anything makes him even more stupid.

Six years ago he tried to instigate a revolution. To usurp me. Six years ago we had a cull. The streets ran red with blood. My men's blood. And my little brother fled like the cowardly shit that he is.

And now he's back.

Only this time none of my men will die. None of my kingdom will crumble. The only thing torn to pieces will be Roman when I finally get my dues.

I sigh, pulling my phone and log in to see what Eleri's up to.

I placed camera's in our suite. She made sure to note all the locations as I did it. It's not that I suspect her of anything, it's not that I'm concerned of what she'll get up to while I'm at work but I like to check-in, to watch her, and to make sure above all that she's safe.

As the screen loads my eyes widen. She's sat on the stairs, facing the main camera.

Completely and utterly naked.

My little jezebel has been waiting for me by the looks of it.

She smiles as if she knows I'm watching and then I remember the tiny light these cameras have, that flash when I'm accessing them.

She opens her legs more, her body angled perfectly for me to watch.

And then she lets out a long moan as she starts touching herself. I'm lucky to turn the volume down before anyone else picks up on what I'm watching because I made sure these new cameras have audio recording.

But I get up, walking out the room, heading to the toilets and lock myself in a cubicle. If my woman is putting on a show I want to enjoy every second of it, and that includes hearing her wanton cries as she makes her cum for me.

She's rocking her body, plunging her fingers into herself. I undo my pants, get my rock hard dick out and start rubbing myself as I watch her.

God this woman does crazy things to me. Insane things.

I never thought she'd be so sexual, so confident, at least not this soon. I thought I'd have to tease it out of her, build her back up but I'm more than happy to realise that part of her was bubbling under the surface waiting to make an appearance this entire time.

And what an appearance.

Her cunt is open, dripping, her body is shaking, I think she might just squirt for me and I watch as her hands move so fast, she's desperate now, she's half screaming as her need takes over and then she slams her head back before it crashes into the stares and she writhes, moaning, screaming, cuming everywhere.

My jezebel. My wanton queen.

I stare at the pool dripping down the steps. She has squirted. My angel has done it again.

I rub myself harder, I'm close too and seeing her release makes me only want mine more. I imagine her mouth, her body right here, sprawled and ready to be used, ready to be filled and I groan as my dick spurts out so hard it hits the wall opposite.

I slump against the cubicle door. Maybe I should stop worrying about my brother because this girl right here might be the death of me long before anyone else is.

"Nico." Preston says calling into the room.

"What?" I reply.

"You're needed." He says as if he doesn't know what's gone on, as if the sounds of Eleri cuming through the phone haven't been echoing about this cold sterile space.

"Coming." I say ignoring the irony of that statement.

CHAPTER
Thirty

He walks through the door and there's a glint in his eye.

"Good day?" I ask before licking the spoon. I'd been eating ice cream before he arrived and now that he's here I'm making a point of being more sexy about it.

"Not really."

"No?" I reply arching my eyebrow.

"Nope, just the same shit." He says walking up to me.

"Huh?" I smirk. He's teasing me, I know it. I saw the light come on, I knew he was logged in. Hell I'd sat there for a full ten minutes, completely starkers waiting for the man because I got too horny and needed an outlet.

"Oh there was one thing." He says dipping his finger into the bowl and scooping out some cream like a heathen before licking

ELLIE SANDERS

it off as I imagine exactly what else he could be doing with the devilish tongue right now.

"What was that?" I ask.

"Well I logged in earlier and saw some very disturbing activity." He murmurs.

"How disturbing?"

"So bad I had to immediately stop what I was doing and take action."

I bite my lip. "I hope the action was appropriate."

"I think the punishment should be." He says.

"Punishment?" I say but I barely get it out because he's grabbing me, hauling me off my chair and half ripping my clothes off.

"Nico." I cry.

"Do you enjoy taunting me?" He says as his mouth begins to devour my flesh.

"Yes." I gasp.

"Do you get some sort of perverse pleasure out of it?"

"I do Nico. I fucking do." I say as his hands remove the last of my clothing except for crotchless panties I decided to treat him to. Only he hasn't discovered what they are yet.

His face is too busy feasting on my breasts to go any lower and I rock my hips against him, feeling the delicious hardness of his cock. This man is just as insatiable as I am and I love the fact he's not shaming me for it, not making me feel like I need to be more chaste.

And what I love more is how he seems to worship my body. Worship my curves.

His hands are kneading my breasts, squeezing them as he groans incomprehensible words.

And then he's laying me down like a sacrificial lamb at his altar. And god what a way to die.

I grin spreading my legs, letting him see the prize.

202

"What are these?" He says getting on his knees.

"Crotchless panties." I say glancing down, making sure the edges are lining up, highlighting how wet I am for him.

"Crotchless panties." He says as it grumbles in his chest. "From now on these are the only panties you wear." He leans over me, his hot breath hitting my skin as I do my best to lie still and not just start humping him. "That is if you wear any panties at all."

I laugh but my laughter dies on my lips as his mouth drops to my clit and he's sucking, licking, rolling so urgently I have to grab his head.

His fingers slip inside and then he starts pumping furiously away as his mouth brings me closer and closer and suddenly I'm cuming, screaming, kicking as he sits back and watches me fall apart.

But he barely gives me time to get my breath back before he's picking me up, carrying me to the bathroom and shoving me face down over the side of the bath. He pours cold liquid over my entire ass and pussy and then he pulls my head up by my hair so that I'm facing myself in the mirror.

"You're going to watch." He says undoing his belt, freeing his incredible dick. "You're going to watch as I fuck your ass."

"Nico. I've never..." I gasp. "I've not done anal before you."

He pauses and then a grin creeps across his face. "Do you want me to go easy on you?" He asks tauntingly. It's not like he hasn't already fucked me in the ass anyway, but the last time was so brutal, so sudden, and yet now that I'm meeting his eyes in the glass I know what I want. I know exactly what I want.

"I never want you to go easy." I say.

"Fuck woman." He groans before plunging his dick into me. I cry out. It hurts. Just like last time but maybe he does heed my words because he is slower, gentler, at least to start with, before he picks up pace, his face contorting as he concentrates in drilling into me, in getting his own satisfaction from this moment.

The bath side sticks into my hips, it's uncomfortable, as is the way he's gripping my hair, holding my head by it but I don't care. I'd rather he pulled every single strand out than he stop right now.

His hand slips down and I feel his fingers sliding into my pussy. I moan loudly. The contrast feels so good.

"You like that Eleri?" He says.

"I fucking love it." I half shout back making sure to make eye contact with him through the mirror. My tits are bouncing, my whole body is shaking and behind I can see the beautiful Adonis of a man glistening in sweat.

"Yeah you do, you filthy little whore." He says before he starts pounding into me, matching each thrust in my ass to each thrust of his fingers. I'm moaning, I'm writhing, I'm right on the edge again and I can see from the way he's straining that he's about to cum too.

"Nico." I cry as my body gives in and he grunts jerking, filling me up entirely before letting my head drop.

He steps back, wiping his dick and stares at where I'm still laid presented for him. And then he walks out coming back seconds later with his phone and takes a picture.

"The fuck?" I say.

He grins. "I'm going to get this printed, blown up, I'll hang it behind my desk for everyone to appreciate."

"The hell you will." I say as I slide off and sit on the cold tile floor.

"Your ass is a masterpiece. Your cunt is too." He states.

I shake my head. He can't be serious. There's no way he is.

He helps me to my feet then tells me to clean up.

Apparently he has work to do and he's gotten his entertainment for the moment. Not that I'm complaining mind. I'm more than happy to be his distraction as many times as he needs. But when I walk into his office twenty minutes later with a coffee for him, he's sat, arms crossed obviously waiting for me.

"What took you so long?" He asks.

"I thought you needed to work."

He grins. "I do but that doesn't mean I don't like a little background music."

I raise my eyebrow? What the hell does that mean exactly? He gets up taking the coffee and sips it before putting it on the side.

His hands tug at the tie around my waist and he undoes the robe I've put on. I let it fall as he admires me once more. He picks me up, lays me on the coffee table on my back and ties my limbs to each of the legs as I watch his face for any hint of what he's planning now.

"I got you a present." He says holding a box up.

"What is it?" I ask. It's big, way too big for jewellery and from the glint in his eye I'm pretty certain it's got something to do with the fact I'm restrained right now.

He opens it, placing it between my thighs. "If I'm honest it's more of a present to myself." He says before sitting down back at his desk.

"What?" I begin as he holds a remote up and then the thing comes to life, it's a robot, a fucking vibrator robot thing. I know my jaw drops as it slides into me.

"What do you think?" He says as I let out a moan in shock and pleasure too.

It's pumping away now, slowly, I hate to admit it but it's pretty fucking hot, and the way Nico is watching, grinning, hell that only makes it better.

"I thought you had work?" I say again.

"I do." He says dropping his gaze focusing on the paperwork in front of him as if I'm not being fucked right now, as if his vibrator thing is not getting me closer and closer and then it stops.

I let out a small moan and he grins, meeting my eye, waiting until he's certain my orgasm has died completely before he turns it back on. The bastard is edging me right now. And there's nothing I can do to stop it.

"Moan for me. Don't hold back. I want to hear how much you like it." He says and god help me I do. I don't even mean to but as it builds again I'm moaning, rocking my hips as much as I can, enjoying every second.

He grins. I think I'm a radio to him right now, a symphony of noise, the perfect backdrop to keep him focused as he stares at whatever the hell paper is apparently more important than me.

I feel my sweat dripping from my brow, I'm close again. I'm moaning more and just as my body shudders, just as my release hits me it stops. It falters. Everything is still.

"Nico." I gasp.

"No Eleri, I need to work."

"Then why won't you let me cum and we can stop this?" I say.

He grins. "Where would be the fun in that?" He hits the button and the toy is vibrating again, pounding into me.

I moan, I writhe, fuck if he can tease me I can tease him too.

His phone rings and he picks it up, his eyes trained on me as he speaks.

I let out a long moan and he grins, turning the remote up more, increasing the intensity which only makes me moan more.

"..no I'm not fucking right now Preston." Nico says. "Eleri is simply providing some stress relief." He says.

I moan again, I don't even mean too but the way this toy is fucking me makes it hard to be silent.

Nico laughs. I don't know if it's because of me or because of something Preston has said but in this moment I don't really care. I shut my eyes, focusing on the pleasure, focusing on the fact I'm spread eagled for this mob boss to do what he wants and by god do I fucking love it.

At some point Nico hangs up and then he's stood over me, watching as I'm getting fucked. He kneels down, teasing my nipples before running his thumb over my bottom lip. I suck it in, lick it. I'm so deeply lost in my own arousal I'm not even aware of what I'm doing.

He grins letting me suck as if I'm pretending it's his cock and in truth I am. I'd love him to unzip his pants and reward me with it right now.

As if he can read my mind he does it, he unzips and gets it out. My mouth waters at the sight of it. He looks so engorged, so turned on.

"Do you want this Eleri?" He says.

I nod. Eagerly.

"Of course you fucking do." He says straddling my chest crushing me as he half forces his cock in my mouth. I moan, I suck. I love every second. He's just so dominant, so aggressive, so uninhibited.

He face fucks me for a few minutes. I'm desperate for him to cum, to fill my mouth with his delicious seed but he pulls out and a trail of saliva drips from the tip of him down onto my chest.

I glance down then back at him. He's pumping away now, getting himself closer and closer.

He moves as he does it and then he's covering me in his cum, covering what feels like my entire torso.

I moan again. I want to cum so desperately but I can see from his face he's not done with me. He won't grant me my own release just yet.

He spreads his cum, covers me in it and then he sits back down, in his big executive leather chair and watches as the machine fucks me some more.

God this man is incredible.

"I love you." I say as I stare back at him. It's true, I do love him. I love everything about him. I love that he's dangerous, I love that he's toxic. I love that he does what he wants to me and he doesn't apologise, I love the way he makes me feel, but most of all, I love the fact that he's mine.

He tilts his head. Pushing the button, increasing the speed and finally, mercifully he lets me cum too.

I scream out his name, I writhe, his cum is dripping off me as I do and I know I'm making a mess everywhere but I don't care, in this moment I want him to see what he's done to me, to witness the effect he has on me.

When I'm done I realise he's back, beside me again.

"Nico." I murmur his name, my voice too hoarse to properly work now. He unties my body but I lay still all the same.

"Tomorrow we are meeting with my brother." He says stroking my face.

My eye widens. Whatever the hell he has planned, whatever the hell is going on, I feel like tomorrow will be an end to it all.

"You need to do exactly what I tell you." He says.

I nod. "I'll do anything." I say. "Anything you need."

"I know you will." He says kissing my forehead. "Because you're such a good girl for me."

I nod again. I am. I am good. I'm his woman and I will make him proud.

He starts whispering, telling me his instructions. I frown listening, trying not to argue with him, telling myself to trust him as he explains his plan.

Him

CHAPTER
Thirty-One

Everything is set.

In less than an hour Eleri will be getting in the car. Wearing the dress I chose, allowing herself to be taken right in the vipers nest.

I feel a pang of guilt, of concern too, because she's putting herself at risk, putting her very life at risk and if she makes a mistake, if I've made a mistake, if I've overlooked something then it's her that will suffer the consequences.

But I haven't. I know I haven't. Everything will go according to plan. Something in my gut tells me that.

And anyway, if I were to keep her here, if I were to work this another way they'd only come for her at the hotel. Because the day I made her my queen, I made her a target. And though I don't regret it right now I wonder if a better man would have protected their woman better.

"They're waiting." Preston says quietly and I look around. I've been sat in the car, aware we've come to a stop for a while and yet my thoughts were on my woman. When today is over I am going to show her exactly what she means to me. Reward her in ways that will blow her mind.

I can see them, the people stood, frowning, fearful, unsure as to what the hell is going on.

I grunt in reply, opening the door and step out. A few of them nod their heads, avert their eyes. It's a sign of respect but right now it feels like treachery, because we know what they've been up to. That they've been working with Emerson.

Blaine is there, with some of my other men, stood behind them and as the women and children are brought out the men on their knees start begging.

"Enough." I snap.

The women are crying now, the children too. They huddle together and my men have to work to keep them all separated, to keep the innocents from the traitors.

"You've been working against me." I say loud enough to carry over the noise.

Some of them shout. Some of them plead.

"Do not deny it. I already have enough evidence." Too much evidence really. It was too easy to find the breadcrumbs, as if Emerson was happy for this family to be his sacrifice.

One of them men falls on his hands. My stomach turns but I am not devoid of mercy.

"You want forgiveness?" I murmur.

He nods.

I pinch my trousers, pulling the fabric up to give myself enough freedom to squat in front of his face.

"What will you give me in exchange."

"Anything you want." He says.

"I want loyalty." I snap.

"I will give you that."

I let out a laugh. "You said that before. You promised me that before."

"I will give you it. We all will."

The other men nod. The women plead again.

Blaine shakes his head behind them. He wants me to kill them. To make an example and while I'm inclined too, these people are not my real enemy.

I look at the children. Some of them are so small they can barely stand and they sit in the dirt. What sort of man would I be if I took my vengeance out on babies?

"I will make you a deal." I say. "You promise my loyalty and yet you have spat in my face." I pause to look back at the men. "So now I ask for you to prove it."

"Anything." One of them shouts.

"You will go to warehouses, to the ones that Emerson controls and you will tell the people there that those businesses have been forfeited. That they are mine now. You will take them for me. You will kill anyone that opposes you. Do I make myself clear?"

They nod. "And when you are done you will come back here. If you do this then I will spare you."

Blaine shakes his head.

The men get up off the ground and I watch as they collect their things, as they begin to follow my orders.

I look over at Preston seeing the surprise on his face. "What?"

"Mercy is not your usual style Nico."

"No." I agree. "But we have bigger fish to fry, and besides we need those factories. Why risk our own men when I can have these do it?"

"You think it will make them loyal?" He scoffs.

"Once Emerson is gone it won't matter." I murmur. "He was the cause of their disloyalty. Cut the head of the snake off and the beast is dealt with."

"Talking of beasts…" Preston mutters checking his phone as it buzzes.

"What?" I ask.

"Your brother is on his way to the party."

I grunt. If Roman is then Eleri will be too. The trap is set. I just hope she is strong enough to survive it.

Her

CHAPTER
Thirty-Two

I step out of the car, ignoring the literal churning of my stomach, and take a moment to smooth out my long black satin dress. Nico picked it, he's picked everything I'm wearing right down to the ruby at my throat and the bracelet around my wrist. It feels like a chain, a handcuff in this moment, but we both know what it's purpose is.

Nico isn't here. I'm alone.

Standing, no staring up at the huge building in front of me. There are pillars across the front making it look more like a temple than a home and yet that's what this is. Nico's family home. The Morelli House.

The sandstone glints in the sunlight and I wonder briefly how much it must have cost to have it imported but the Morelli family aren't exactly strapped for cash and no doubt his grandfather thought it was worth the expense.

Someone steps out through the huge front doors and I let out a long, low breath to calm myself. Just do as he said, I tell myself, 'Do everything he told me to and by the time the sun comes up tomorrow Nico will have gotten his revenge. He will have annihilated all of the men who are plotting against him.'

"Welcome." The man says as I begin to climb the steps up, holding my dress to aid me.

"I'm…" I begin but he cuts across me.

"I know who you are. My nephew has already informed me."

I nod. So this is Constantine Morelli. Nico's uncle. His father's brother. A shrewd man, a smart man, but one who was happy to take orders, not give them, if the rumours are to be believed. When Nico's father was murdered, it was his mother who took on the other families, not Constantine, though he was there by her side, she was the one giving orders.

And when she was murdered, it was Nico who stood up, who became head of the family. And Constantine once again only had a support role.

"You are not what I expected." Constantine says holding his hand for mine and I offer it more to be polite. He raises it to his lips, kissing as if we were in ancient times, as if I really were his queen.

"What were you expecting?" I ask. No doubt Roman has already informed them all of what I am, what I look like. How marred my face is.

He takes a moment to study me, to look at the scar and then he meets my eye. A small grin threatens to take his lips. "You are like fire *mio cara*." He murmurs.

I frown at the words. I don't know Italian. I don't speak any languages but my native tongue and in this moment I wish I did because if they all switch to it, to Italian, I'll be sat like an idiot not understanding a word.

"The others are downstairs." He says. "Let's get a drink while we wait."

I nod. He hasn't asked where Nico is and I don't know if he knows his plan but I'm not going to say anything.

He leads me into the house. It feels even more like a temple inside. The floors are marble, there are pillars inside too, four either side, running through the hallway drawing your eye to the very end where there's another great door. The walls are painted with white but along the very top, far above my head is an intricate pattern that I know even from this angle is made from gold leaf.

I want to ask why the house looks like this, they're Italian, not Greek and yet I bite my tongue, keep my questions to myself. I need to stick to the plan, play the obedient, almost docile lover until Nico arrives with his grand finale.

We walk through, our steps echoing in the space because there is nothing but hard surfaces to soak up the noise. Constantine doesn't speak so I don't either. His grip on my arm is firm but not hard, it's as if he is leading me to a dance, and in a way I guess that's what this will be, a melee of sorts, a grand opera of Nico's creation.

We step down a winding staircase, it's hard to walk side by side and Constantine lets me go first though in truth I'd rather follow. As we descend it feels like we're no longer above the ground, that suddenly we're in a cave, a subterranean expanse created far below the depths of the house.

I wait at the very bottom and Constantine smiles as he steps beside me.

Ahead is a great table. There are huge candelabras, all flickering with firelight. And in front of all twenty four, no twenty six chairs, a place has been set, with silver cutlery laid out, crystal glasses, as if we were about to sit down to a feast.

I let myself look then, I let my eye fall on the other people, the countless faces all watching me with what feels like a mix of amusement and fascination.

I don't recognise any of them. Not that I expected too but right now I feel like I'm in the lion's den and I'm a snake they're about to rip to pieces.

"So this is the girl?" A woman says stepping out from the mass of suits. Everyone is dressed in their finery. There are only two other women, though both are notably older than me.

"This is Eleri." Constantine says. "Nico's partner."

The woman smirks, just a little, stepping closer, taking me in. "He does have a type." She murmurs.

"What does that mean?" I ask before I can stop myself.

Her eyes twinkle. "Your body is like hers." She says and then her eyes fall on my face. "But the rest of you..." She frowns.

"That's enough Carla." Constantine mutters and her eyes flit to him.

"He hasn't been with a woman in over six years." Carla states. "Beyond simply fucking them that is. Is it not right to compare them? The old queen with the new?"

Constantine makes a noise, it sounds like a growl, deep in his throat.

I narrow my eyes, she's goading me, in a small way, she's testing me to see if I match to whoever the hell this 'old queen' was.

"Let's get our guest a drink." Constantine says leading me away from her prying eyes.

"Not exactly a guest though is she?" She says. "This is still Nico's home after all."

Constantine stiffens slightly but doesn't take the bait and mercifully we reach the drinks table with no more comments. But everyone else is watching me still. I can feel their eyes running over me, over my skin, over my body, but most of all I can feel them trying to get a good look at my face, trying to catch a glimpse before looking away as if I might just turn them to stone.

A few are muttering. The woman is back amongst them and a small group breaks off, walking to take their places. Nico was very specific about where I was to sit and as I watch them from the corner of my eye I see no one has taken my place. Did I expect them too? To challenge me? To challenge Nico, because no doubt he's told them all where they're place is too. I guess I'm relieved no one has. That his authority stands even when he's not present.

Constantine hands me a glass of wine. The colour is so red it looks like blood and as I take a sip I half expect it to taste like blood too. We go to sit and I'm infinitely aware of what I need to do. What my instructions were.

Around me everyone is talking, it sounds like they're catching up, as if these people haven't been together, in one space for a long time. No one is talking to me. Constantine is sat too far to engage me in any sort of conversation though he is glancing at me every so often as if he's checking to make sure I'm okay. I take the opportunity to drink, to finish my glass.

And then I get up, going to refill it.

Again no one is paying me any attention. Apparently the initial excitement of my presence has worn off and now that they've all had a good gawp at me they're happy to pretend I don't exist. And in all honesty, right now I'm happy to let them.

I walk back to the table, there's one big carafe of wine. The jug is huge, made of crystal, and I fear I don't have the strength to lift it but in this instance, it's my secondary concern. I glance back, just for a moment to make sure no one is watching and as I do my fingers find the bracelet, slowly twisting the tiny vial that's disguised as jewel.

It comes apart easily enough and I pinch the glass between my thumb and forefinger before tipping the contents into the wine.

And then, as practised as any thief I screw the vial back into its place.

My heart is pounding as I do it. And though I'm not trembling I've no idea how I'm even holding my nerve right now. I wait a second hoping the liquid has mixed well enough and try to raise the carafe only it's so heavy I can barely lift it.

"Let me help with that." An only too familiar voice says and I jump slightly as he stands beside me.

He's smirking, amused. For a moment I wonder how long he's been stood, and whether I've fucked up, whether he's seen what I've done but surely he would call me out if that was the case?

He picks up the crystal and pours out some wine into my glass before filling a second.

And then he's back, eyes focused on me.

"Tell me Eleri, where is my brother?" He asks quietly.

"He's running late." I reply.

He snorts. Nico never runs late. Nico is the very epitome of time itself.

He takes a sip of his wine, staring at my scar. "I did some research into you." He says. "After our last encounter."

"And what did you discover?" I reply. I'll be damned if I let him bully me, frighten me, show me up and especially as it feels like a lot of the bodies seated around the table are now watching us intently.

"You were a singer. Not a bad one, and then something happened, your face…" He flicks his hand almost flamboyantly to gesture at me. "After that you began working at one of my brother's establishments."

I blink but don't respond. It wasn't 'something' that happened. It was 'someone' and besides, it is over now, I've had my revenge. Nico gave me that.

He narrows his eyes. "I think you would have been quite lovely before." He drops them, staring unashamedly at my breasts, at my hips before looking back up. "Just as lovely as Rosa."

"Who?" I ask. It was a stupid thing to say. He's dropped the name on purpose and even as the words leave my lips I realise who he meant, who the other woman alluded too.

"His first queen. The one he had killed." Roman says and my heart for a second stops, completely freezes in my chest.

"Excuse me?"

"He didn't tell you about her?" He says grinning. "But of course he didn't. How very like Nico to keep secrets. No doubt he's sent you ahead, to prepare the scene, to do his dirty work."

"He's done no such thing." I say quickly. Too quickly.

He lets out a low laugh. "If I were to strip that dress from you right now, what are the odds you have some sort of weapon on you? A gun, a blade perhaps hidden amongst those delicious curves?"

"If you lay a hand on me…" I begin and he laughs a little louder.

"*Rilassarsi.*" He murmurs. "I will deal with Nico first and then perhaps you won't be so unwilling."

I snarl. The fuck is he talking about?

"Roman." Constantine says loudly. He's close enough to have heard our conversation though I don't know how long he's been stood there.

Roman looks across at him. "Dear uncle." He says. "How very predictable for you to play the protector, especially when the man who should is noticeably absent."

"Nico will be here soon." I say because the way he's said it makes it sound like Nico won't show, that he's either afraid too or he's been indisposed of and god help me I hope that's not the case.

"Sure he will." Roman replies. "But in the meantime, we might as well make ourselves as comfortable as we can." He picks up the carafe, carrying it past me and Constantine, and walks over to where everyone else is seated. "Let's enjoy my brother's hospitality." He says pouring it out, filling everyone's glasses, even those who haven't got empty ones. "For as long as it lasts."

I glance at Constantine and he gives me a reassuring look which I return before taking my seat at the very head once more.

Roman is still making a play of being host but his eyes keep flickering to me. God I hope Nico gets here soon because the wolves are circling. And the rabid one is practically foaming at the mouth.

Constantine sits back down. Everyone is seated now. I drink more wine. I keep drinking, even though I know what's in it. What it will do.

Roman sits three chairs down from me. It's not his place. Not the one Nico designated for him but he's clearly not moving and he makes a play of staring right at me, his eyes boring into my face, meeting me head on as he too sips his wine.

I half glare back at him. Perhaps it's the alcohol that gives me the courage, perhaps it's something worse but as we face each other off I feel it, the slowly icy chill slipping in through my veins. The way my body is getting heavy. I move my finger, just a tiny bit and the effort almost makes me sweat.

I look back up, meeting Roman's eyes once more. He's frowning now, staring at my hand and I see the tiniest imperceptible movement that tells me he's feeling it too.

The poison is working.

We're all turning to stone.

CHAPTER
Thirty-Three

This place used to haunt me. Used to haunt my every waking moment. I haven't been near it in years and I haven't stepped foot inside in even longer.

I see the name, my family name, carved into the sandstone above the door. It should fill me with a sense of pride, as sense of honour. Our family home. The hallowed halls where our name became something of worth, where our power, our destinies were formed. Where we became kings.

And yet this place feels like a tomb.

So I guess it's fitting that this is where I will vanquish my demons, put them to the sword and bury them for all eternity.

I clench my fists taking each step slowly as I make my way inside.

The house is quiet. So quiet.

There are over two dozen people sat in the catacombs beneath me and yet it feels like I am the only one living. The only mortal.

Preston, Blaine, all my men wait outside. We've already started the avalanche, though the people inside don't know it. We've already taken retribution on every single family who's betrayed us and in a few minutes I'm going to watch as this fact sinks in to them.

But this moment now is all me. No henchmen, no backup, just me. My hand that takes revenge. My hand that deals the death blow.

Because by god have I waited long enough for this.

I walk down the staircase descending into what feels like the abyss. I already know exactly who is waiting for me. The few surviving members of my father's family. The heads of all the other houses too. I summoned each and everyone. I made it clear no excuses were to be had. If they failed to show I would butcher them in their homes.

Emerson is here. As is his cousin. His brother is no doubt still recovering from what Blaine did to him.

And my own brother is here. Sat at this very moment at the same table as the person I care most about.

Eleri.

Even now, even though I know this is the best way to ensure success, the thought that I have risked her life, have even considered it makes me more angry than I can articulate. And the thought that she is sat within touching distance of Roman after what he did to my last queen… I shake my head.

This is the only way. I know it. And besides she agreed. She was willing.

I take my last step, I hear it echo and I smirk looking around at everyone sat.

It's almost like a photo, a picture perfect cut out scene before me. Everyone sat, still, waiting for me. I look at them, walk around, take my time to study each and every one. Loyal servant and traitor alike, I stare at them all with the same look on my face until I reach the head, where my queen is.

Her eye is on me. It's the only part of her body that she can move. I tilt my head, taking in her frame. She's so expressive. Even now, even frozen, I can feel my body wanting her, yearning for her and I can feel her need for me too.

But she isn't begging. As immobile as she is, as much as her very survival right now depends on the vial safe within my pocket, she's waiting for me. Patiently. Obediently. Even my old queen wouldn't have behaved as such, wouldn't have been as loyal and perhaps that should have been a marker. A sign of what was to come. How easily Roman would seduce her to his side and how it would all end in blood.

Her blood.

Like a fucking Greek tragedy if ever there was one.

Star crossed lovers. That was what the note had said. How Roman had classed them and in a way I guess they were. Only she didn't understand what her actions actually meant. That is until she walked into this very room and saw my mother, laid out on the floor, her blood pouring from the wound at her throat, like an unholy sacrifice to the gods of greed.

And when she did realise, I guess drowning herself in the lake must have been the only logical next step. Because she would have known I would have killed her. For all my love, for all my want for her, she betrayed me, and worse, she let my mother bear the consequences and for that I would never forgive.

My hand slides into my pocket. I grasp the vial and as I pull it out her eye flickers to it. She knows that just one drop is enough to give her what she needs. To give her my salvation.

"Your wine was laced with a poison." I state. "It works by overriding your body, overriding your muscles, and eventually it will stop your heart."

Eleri doesn't react. She just watches me, still waiting.

"There is only one antidote. One form of salvation." I say turning to look at everyone else for a moment. "Without this, you have four hours at the most to live."

Eyes move, that's all I get. Pupil dilation. No other gestures but it's enough to tell me that every one of these men and women are petrified. There's a ticking clock above their heads and I am the only one who can spare them.

I open the vial slowly, careful not to spill it because it's more than just her life that depends on this holy elixir.

I let a tiny drop fall on my finger and as I do I know every other person sat, frozen, immobile, is watching the action. I run the liquid over my own lips, let it coat them and I can taste the slight bitter taste.

"My queen." I murmur as I lower my face to hers she shuts her eye. And as my lips touch hers I feel it, the hardness, the iciness, the poison that has turned her body to stone slowly start to change. To melt. Her skin warms, her lips move just a fraction, and my tongue instinctively dives into her mouth, claiming her even as she's coming back to life.

She lets out a moan, her tongue wraps around mine and as her hand reaches up to cup my face I grasp it holding her to me as I devour her very essence with my kiss.

I break away, not because I want to but because there are others I must save before the poison goes too far.

She lets out a low breath, leaning back into the chair, watching as I walk around the table choosing who I will spare and who I will sacrifice. Constantine of course I save. My uncle has been a loyal soldier. Carla, head of the La Perla Family I save too. Though she's got a mouth, and a big one at that, I know she hasn't done anything close to warrant execution. Hell, she was the first to come to me, months ago, when the first plot to usurp me was formed.

I save a few more. Those who are useful, and those who deserve it. But the rest…

I turn, looking at them, at Emerson, at Jace, at all the heads of the other families, families that after tonight will no longer exist. And then finally my eyes settle on him.

On my brother.

Though his face is frozen he's still got his signature smirk, as if he knew what was happening in the last few moments before he lost all control, and he set his face to an expression he thought would annoy me the most. Only it doesn't. Not this time.

I let out a laugh. His eyes move a tiny bit but beyond that there is nothing.

I pick up a glass. It's half full and I take a sniff. The poison is odourless, colourless, tasteless. Completely undetectable.

I tilt the glass, letting the wine pour out dramatically onto the floor where it splashes.

I can tell Roman wants to say something. A few others do too. I see Emerson's eyes flit to his cousin and then across the table to my brother.

"Tonight you came here to witness a downfall." I say. My voice echoes around the space and I wait a moment until it goes quiet. "Like vultures you thought you could sit at my table, enjoy my hospitality, and then pick at my carcass."

Eleri shifts, narrowing her eye. I can see from her expression that she is more than ready for this to get going. That clearly they didn't treat my queen with the respect she is due.

"Only that's not how this is going to go." I murmur. "Six years ago my family was betrayed. By my own brother." I state.

A few of the men I've saved react. Not many people know the tale, and I guess it's a fault on my part. I allowed my pride to taint my judgement, and I allowed my childhood love for my sibling override the actions of what the man grew up to be.

And now we are all here witnessing the consequences. Suffering. Just as my mother did.

"Maria Morelli was murdered by that man." I say pointing to him. Pointing to Roman. "He thought in killing her he could stage a revolt, place the blame on me and take over as head." I state looking at each of their faces, seeing in whose eyes the shock is, and in whose there is no reaction beyond complicity.

"He lured her here, to her own home, and he had his henchmen butcher her like a dog." I snap.

"Rosa was the reason she came here." Constantine says and I shake my head.

"Rosa was as fooled by him, as were many others in this room. But tonight you will pay for your crimes." I reply.

Roman makes a noise, the tiniest impartible sound but it's as if he's choking. I narrow my eyes.

"I believe my brother would like to speak." I say walking over to him and slowly I pull out some ties, binding him to his seat.

As I kneel beside him I look up, for once not seeing the boy I climbed trees with, not seeing the boy I would play fight with, the boy I would race against around the house. I see the man, the monster, the murderer.

When his ties are tight I stand up, taking the vial once more and let a tiny bit of antidote grace his lips.

His face relaxes, he starts to regain movement and then he jerks against his restraints.

"No little brother." I murmur. "There is no escape this time. No reprieve."

"I didn't murder her." Roman shouts. "It was Rosa, she did it."

A few of the men hiss. Roman glances at them and I glance too. Perhaps Roman forgets everyone that he invited, perhaps in his absence he has forgotten the bloodlines because Rosa's family are here. Her father is here. Sat right opposite Roman and though the two of us share an uneasy alliance since his daughter's demise I've given him the antidote nonetheless.

"Rosa would never do such a thing." He snarls.

"She did it. She said she would unite our families. That together we would run them." Roman says.

I shake my head. "Rosa was not like that. Rosa would never have said those things." I state. "She betrayed me only because of you. She died only because of you."

"And yet you've replaced her so easily." Roman taunts looking at Eleri who even now is sat, silent, observing everything without needing to speak.

I look at her. At my queen. I wonder what she must think of these revelations. Does she even know who Rosa is? I've certainly never spoken about her, in truth not thought about her in years and yet here she is being openly discussed as if she were the love of my life, as if Eleri means nothing.

"Eleri is nothing like Rosa." I say.

Carla snorts. "She looks like her. Same shape body…"

"She is nothing like her." I snap. "Eleri has never betrayed me. Eleri will never betray. She was the one who poisoned the wine. She drank it herself, knowing exactly what it was, knowing that it could kill her and trusting that I would save her."

A few people react to that. To the fact that Eleri was the one who poisoned them. And that she willingly put her life on the line. Willingly sacrificed herself for me.

Eleri shifts in her seat, meeting each and every one of their glances. My perfect fucking queen.

"Poison is a woman's tool." Roman spits. "No man would resort to such a thing."

"No brother. It is our family's." I reply surprised he has such poor knowledge of our ancestry. I look around, so many of them here do not know, do not understand us, the Morelli's at all.

"The Morelli's are not just an old bloodline, but an ancient one. We are descended from Borgia. Lucrezia herself is our great grandmother many times removed. So it is more than fitting is it not that we revert back to the old ways, our original family's way of conducting business?"

A few people flinch. Lucrezia is enough of a legend even these days to make people uncomfortable but I am not ashamed of who I am, where I came from.

I look back at Roman. He's glaring at me. Emerson is glaring too, or at least as much as he can with the limited movement his body can make.

I pull a knife from my suit jacket. "As much as this has been riveting I think it's time we got on with it."

I walk behind one of the other men, in truth not one of the big players, but he was the man who ambushed our van, he was the one responsible for luring me away so that others could ransack my house and take Eleri.

I could just leave him, and the others too, let them stay here, stuck like statues until the poison finishes the job, but what satisfaction is there to be had in that? None, that's what. And besides, it's not nearly enough for the revenge I want, the revenge I need. The revenge my mother's blood calls for.

I lift the blade, sliding it like butter across his throat and his blood spurts out, like a fountain, cascading over the table, over the glasses, and the people around him.

A few people gasp. Carla has the gall to shriek but my eyes are on Eleri who's smiling at me. Encouraging me almost to finish this.

"You may have been wondering why I took so long to get here." I say, swiping the blade against the next man's throat. He dies in a similar manner. "While you were guzzling my wine, while the poison was working its way through your system, I myself and my men were working to eradicate all the families who have opposed me. Every man here frozen, every man here, waiting to die will do so knowing they've condemned their families too. That their wives, and their children will suffer for what they've done."

I drag the blade again. Another man's blood spurts forth.

I reach Emerson and his eyes dart to my brother. I let out a low laugh.

"He cannot save you. Whatever lies he spun, whatever paradise he promised you, there is nothing for you but my mercy." I say lowering my face to his ear. "Only I have none."

I can hear his breathing, as much as the poison is slowing his body down his fear and adrenaline is trying to make his heart race.

"You once said you would enjoy watching my downfall. I guess the same is true of me. Goodbye Emerson." I murmur before slicing his throat.

Jace is next. Then another man. I move around the table, taking them all out. The people that can move remain as still as they can, only jerking when the blood of someone sprays them.

And then it is me and Roman. My brother and I.

For so long I wanted him dead. I wanted to flay him alive, to make him pay for the way he betrayed our mother and yet when the moment had presented itself last time I found myself wanting. I let my emotions override my judgement. I was a fool and now as I stand here, looking down at him, I realise what a fool I have been.

He has cost me so much. He cost me my first love, he cost me my mother, thousands of men, women and children, all dead and all can be traced back to him. Roman.

"Any last words?" I say to him.

He lets out a laugh. And then he lunges at me. How the hell he got the ties loose I don't know but as his body moves towards me, something flies through the air and it hits him right in the eye.

He slumps back into the chair. He's not dead. He's still obviously breathing.

I turn staring in the direction of where the steak knife came and Eleri is there, hands still gripping the arms of the chair, her eye flashing with something fierce.

"You…" I murmur and she grins. Christ, in that moment I swear my cock comes to life. To see her, covered in blood, her soul on fire, with murder in her eye. She's the most incredible, beautiful, creature I've ever seen.

"Please continue." She says as if she understands, and I realise she does. She knows exactly what this moment feels like because this is what I gave her when I gifted her those men, the ones who tried to destroy her. This is what it feels like, to finally get your revenge.

I incline my head. As my queen commands.

I take the dagger, plunging it into my brother's throat. I don't slice this time. I don't grant him the quick mercy the others were giving, I stab him, right through his oesophagus, and then I pull it out, plunging it into his chest, over and over, stabbing him not just for myself but for my mother too and I guess in a way for Rosa, for the stupid, sweet, naïve and yet deceitful woman that she was.

I stab until my arm screams in protest. I stab until it feels like my own muscles are seizing up and when his body slumps I finally stop. Leaving the knife embedded.

I walk to where Eleri is still sat and I put my hands on the back of her chair, as if it were a throne. Around the table were twenty six places. Twenty five people. Of them only eight remain alive. Only eight who will continue to work for the Morelli family.

Not bad for a day's work.

"From this day on the other families no longer exist. I have taken over their operations, I am now head of their families." I say. "You all have passed the test. You are loyal to me and tomorrow I will distribute out new positions accordingly."

I glance down, from this angle all I can see is the top of Eleri's head. She's not looking at me, she's staring at the people around us.

"The Morelli family does not stand for insults, for traitors, for betrayal. You have been granted a mercy. Any sign of dissent will be treated swiftly and accordingly."

I jerk my head for them to go and they jump up, clearly happy to be leaving. Clearly happy to still be alive.

Eleri gets up, facing me, cupping my face with her hand and I kiss it.

"You were magnificent." I say.

"So were you."

I smirk. "Let's go home."

"I thought this was your home?" She says.

I shake my head. "This place is more of a mausoleum than a home."

She glances at all the dead bodies and in particular my brother. "I guess it is now." She says and I can't help but laugh.

I take her hand, leading her away from all the death. I can feel the wetness of the blood on her skin and I look at her. She looks like a goddess. She looks like an avenging angel.

"Were you not scared?" I ask.

"For a moment." She admits. "Your brother told me about Rosa, he said you killed her. But then I reminded myself of what you've done for me, how you've saved me and I knew you'd never let me down."

My lips curl for a moment at the confidence that she has in me. It's almost outstanding.

"I didn't kill her. Rosa killed herself." I state. "She realised what she'd done, how Roman had seduced her, and that she'd contributed to my mother's death."

She shakes her head. "I'm sorry."

"Don't be. It was a long time ago and besides I've vanquished the ghosts now."

"Yes you have." She says pulling me to her, kissing me hard as if all this death and destruction has turned her on.

"I love you." I say and she lets out a little laugh.

"I know." She replies.

"Shall we go home?"

"Yes." I say. Only she doesn't know we're not going back to the hotel. We're going somewhere else entirely.

CHAPTER
Thirty-Four

"Where are we?" I ask looking around. I don't recognise the roads, the houses, any of this.

"It's a surprise." Nico murmurs.

I roll my eye just as the car comes to a stop. Nico gets out, walks around and opens the door offering his hand for me to take.

"Trust me you're going to like this." He says.

I smile because I do trust him. I trust him with my life.

He holds my hand as we walk down through the ornate garden and towards what looks like a palace.

"Welcome to your new home." Nico says.

"What?"

"I bought this house for us. For new memories. For a new start." He states kissing me and it's hard not to lose myself in it.

"What was wrong with the old house?" I ask. Surely we could have repaired the damage, it wasn't that bad was it?

"It wasn't grand enough for you." He says. "You deserved more."

"No I don't." I say just as Blaine and Preston appear.

Nico looks at them and they both nod as if in unison.

"What is this?" I ask.

"Come Eleri." Nico murmurs taking my hand again, leading me through the house. Inside it's gleaming, white marble is everywhere, the hall way cuts through the entire centre so from the front door you can see out to the veranda beyond. There are huge Crittal glass doors and as they slide open I can see dozens of candles, all flickering against the night. Rose petals have been strewn across the floor.

Nico leads me out and as I stare about he drops to one knee and though I know a millisecond before he does it, I still can't help but gasp.

"Eleri Gordon." He says. "Will you marry me?"

"Yes." I say without hesitation.

He grins pulling out a huge princess shaped ring that he slips so perfectly onto my finger I wonder if he's secretly measured it while I was sleeping.

"My perfect queen." He murmurs.

"My perfect king." I reply.

He kisses me again and we hear both Blaine and Preston applauding in the background. Apparently they both approve, apparently my show of loyalty earlier was enough to finally win them to my side.

As he leads me back inside I know where we're headed, or at least, what we're going to do. The stairs are so ornate, they wind around, splitting into two then come back together again. At the very top I stop to admire the huge crystal chandelier that hangs from the ceiling.

We walk through to the bedroom. Nico has undoubtedly had this restyled to his tastes. It's rich, ornate, but there are the same satin sheets he favours.

"I've had all your things brought across." He says.

"Everything?" I ask.

"Everything." He says smiling. "Including Sarpedon."

I drop his hand, walking through the door to where I assume the walk in wardrobe is and I smile, I think my pet is growing on him after all. As I begin rifling through the drawers Nico appears behind me.

"What are you looking for?" He asks.

"You'll see." I reply. "Give me two minutes."

He shakes his head but he does it, walking back out and I find what I'm looking for. An underwear set he's not seen.

I unzip my dress, discard everything on the floor and pull on the lacy set.

When I walk out he's laid on the bed, in just his boxers. He runs his eyes over me and lets out a low whistle.

"Worth the wait?" I ask.

"Always worth the wait." He says beckoning me over.

I crawl onto the bed. His hands caress me and I rock my hips against the already impressive bulge in his pants.

"You are insatiable aren't you?" He says.

I nod. "For you."

His mouth finds mine just as his hands unhook my bra and my breasts fall so perfectly for him to bury his face in.

I moan as he begins to knead them. The way he worships my body is something else.

My hands slip back, I pull his cock free and start rubbing him.

"That's it Eleri." He groans. "Get me good and ready for you."

I grin. He's always ready for me. Just as I'm always ready for him. I pull his boxers off, slide my panties off too and I straddle him as he watches me intensely.

As I hold his eye contact I slide myself on top of him and we both moan in unison.

"Your cunt is a gift from the gods." He murmurs. "The very gates of Elysium."

Yeah it is.

I roll my hips, putting one hand on his chest and start riding him. He grabs my ass, letting me take control for once and as I fuck him we stare at each other like two souls lost and found. I gyrate against him, letting him slide out before pushing down so that he bottoms out with a thump that makes us both groan.

"Fuck that's good." He mutters.

"It's all yours Nico. All of me." I gasp. "Every inch of me belongs to you."

He grins, grabbing my breasts, holding them as they bounce up and down.

"So fucking perfect." He says.

"Cum with me." I gasp. I'm close now, so close.

He nods. Grabbing my hips, thrusting in time, and together we scream out our release.

I fall on top of him, feeling as his cum pools inside me.

"I love you Nico Morelli." I say. "I love you so much."

"I love you." He replies, sweeping my hair back, staring at my face and I don't flinch, I don't hide I let him look. My soon to be husband and perhaps one day, the father of my children.

THE END

COERCION

A MAFIA ROMANCE

Her

FIVE YEARS AGO MY UNCLE MURDERED MY FAMILY, BUTCHERED THEM in their beds. And I know the only reason I'm alive is because I'm useful, a thing to barter. A thing to sell.

Well, today he'll get his payday. He's made a deal, he's handing me over as a blushing bride to Preston Civello.

I'm meant to be the rubber stamp of a truce between our two warring families but in secret I'm there to bring my new husband down, to bring Nico Morelli down from the inside. To act as a spy.

Only I have an entirely different plan - I'm going to seduce him, to win him to my side. I'll play the good little wife and I'll serve him on my knees if I have to, all the while pretending that my past never happened.

But when all my horrible secrets are revealed, will my husband believe me or will he see me as just a traitor in his bed?

Him

I KNOW HER PAST. I KNOW HER HISTORY. I'M CONVINCED SHE'S GOING to be a snake sleeping in my bed but when my Mafia Princess Bride is all but dragged down the aisle and I clap eyes on her tear-stained face, I don't care. Something feral takes over.

She might have been a pawn in her uncle's games but from now on she belongs to me. She's mine.

Only that's not exactly true because of the promise Nico forced me to make- she doesn't know it but she's his god daughter, and I'm not allowed to touch her. Not allowed to claim her. He's made her off limits, a fruit I'm forbidden from tasting and, as each day passes, it's getting harder and harder to resist my tempting little wife. And tempting she is. Dangerously so.

When all the players come out of the woodwork, I'm forced to face a truth I never thought possible, that maybe she's not as loyal as she seems. Maybe she really is the snake I first took her for.

- Things to know about Coercion:
- Mafia with a healthy dose of spice
- Age Gap
- MF
- Jealous / possessive hero
- Strong female with a traumatic backstory
- Dual POV
- Trigger warning list in front of book

Grab your copy here:
https://www.amazon.com/dp/B0CM7MSP5S/

COERCION
Sneak Peak

Preston

ost men don't dream of their wedding day. Most men don't even consider what it will be like, if they even have one.

But then again, most men aren't in the line of business I am. I stand stiffly with Nico beside me. My parents had an arranged marriage, as did my grandparents. It's nothing unusual with our way of life and yet I'd never considered it for myself. Truth be told I'd never imagined getting married at all.

With death stalking your every move it seems a selfish thing to want to build a family, to want to put others at risk.

Maybe that's why I'm so stoic about this. I'm not leaving some loved one behind, I'm not making some grand sacrifice, in reality this decision was pretty easy to make. This is for the good of the Morelli Family, it's the least I can do considering how much Nico's family have sacrificed for me.

As the music begins to play out I let out a low breath. Nico and I have already agreed how we're going to handle this. It's a marriage of convenience, a way to seal the deal and while I'll smile for the cameras that's all this is; a show. I'll pretend until this alliance falls apart, if it falls apart, and if it doesn't well, at least the girl will have a little more freedom at my side, that is, if she deserves it.

Nico shifts beside me. The church is full. Levi has his side packed as though he really does consider Ruby to his actual offspring. All his men have that trademark diamond pinned to their suit pocket. God knows how much those things cost. Each diamond shows the rank of the man wearing it. The bigger the diamond, the higher up the food chain they are, with Gunnar having a full five carat monstrosity that looks almost ridiculous as it glints under the stained glass window.

On short notice it's our men that fill out the pews to the right making this look even more of a shotgun wedding than it already is.

Behind me I can sense them approaching. I can hear the tell-tale ruffles of a wedding dress, but I can hear something else too, above the music, above the merry little tune that's ringing out around us.

She's crying.

My heart twists. I haven't even laid eyes on her and already I feel something akin to sympathy. God, what has this girl gone through?

I wish I could stop this, I wish I could pull her aside and tell her what's really going on but I can't. Besides, it could all be an act, a way to get me on side, while underneath she's Levi's creature through and through.

But she starts fighting harder, giving up all pretence and as we all watch on I realise she's either the best actress I've ever seen in my life or this is real. She really doesn't want this. She really is fighting as if her life depends upon it.

She digs her heels into the thick carpet and he curls his fist clearly wanting to hurt her but he refrains under all our watchful gaze. Instead, he digs his fingers into her arm and jerks hard enough that she stumbles forward and he can haul her down the last bit to where I'm stood.

As they come up beside me it takes all I have not to punch the bastard in the face but then I look at her, at my bride, and my heart seems to stop.

She has a long veil covering her entirety, underneath a satin dress clings to a curvaceous body that makes my mouth water and my dick come to life. I know Levi said she was twenty one but she looks older.

She looks nothing like the blurry photo he showed me on his phone.

But it's the tears streaming down her beautiful face that seem to captivate me in a way I didn't expect.

She keeps her eyes down, refusing to look at any of us. Levi is gripping her arm in a way that I'm certain will bruise badly and I'm quick to pull her free. In less than an hour she'll belong to me anyway. I'm staking my claim, making him see that from now on she's untouchable to him and all his cronies.

His lips curl as he looks at me and then he slinks away off to sit on the front pew beside Gunnar who is scowling like someone has shat on his bed and made him sleep in it.

The ceremony is quick. Someone clearly bribed the priest because he doesn't seem to care that the bride wants no part of this. When it comes to her vows she stumbles, sobbing harder, too distraught to say any articulate words and Levi gets up, slapping his hand over her mouth from behind and speaks them for her as if none of us would care.

Nico gives me a look and the priest acts like this is all perfectly normal, like every blushing bride behaves like this, as if they have a gun pressed to their temple.

Putting the rings on is even worse. I have to wrench her hand open and practically jam the thing down her finger. The diamonds seem to sparkle in jest, their light catches on the tears still streaming down her cheeks. She doesn't make any attempt to pick up the gold band meant for me and in the end I pick it up and put it on myself.

When he says the words 'man and wife' she seems to deflate more. Like it's a death sentence she's just been handed. Like life as she knows it is over.

I take her hand again, trying to ignore how small it feels in my grasp, and we walk back down the aisle while I glare at every man we pass.

We only have to get through the reception now and then this entire charade is over.

* * *

LEVI AND GUNNAR ARE DRINKING LIKE THIS REALLY IS A CELEBRATION. Eleri is sat stiff with her eyes continuously darting to Ruby who still hasn't looked up. Her veil is off her face, every few seconds she sniffs. Her makeup, that no doubt was immaculate hours ago, is smeared down her cheeks and a part of me wants to scoop her up and take her away from all the jackals surrounding her.

To her left is Levi and then Gunnar. I'm on her right, our chairs placed close enough that my leg should be touching hers and it takes a lot of effort to keep it twisted at an angle so I'm not. Nico is beside me with Eleri placed on the nearest table to ours. I wonder if they did that on purpose, to try to goad Nico. To insult him.

Eleri doesn't make a fuss. She takes her place beside Blaine and they seem to make conversation. If anything I wish I could join them. I bet they're having a far better time than all of us sat on the top table.

It's a five course meal. Each one seems to drag out. I don't speak, I just eat, wanting this damned day over with. I don't think Ruby has more than a bite the entire time. By the time desert comes, Levi is making blatant innuendos about his niece; comments no decent uncle would say.

"She comes from good breeding stock." Levi says slapping Ruby's thigh as she jolts like she's been hit by lightning. "I expect you to use her well, after all, this is about binding our families together."

Ruby physically recoils, only there's nowhere for her to go; she's caught between the brute to her left and me, a man she's never met before and clearly doesn't trust. If I could I'd say something to placate her, to make her feel safe, but Levi is too close. Besides, I don't know what her reaction would be if I did. I can't risk it. I can't do anything but let this insult continue.

"Her mother was easy to train." Gunnar says leaning right over his plate to look me in the eyes. "In time I'm sure you'll get her to behave exactly the way you want. Turn her into a proper whore for you."

I clench my fists at the way they just spoke about my now wife even though she clearly does not want me as a husband.

"Keep it together." Nico mutters beside me, low enough that only I hear.

"Alright for you." I say back through gritted teeth. "Would you do the same if they spoke of Eleri like that?"

Nico tilts his head, his eyes flashing. "The situation is not the same."

"Eleri is your wife just as Ruby is now mine."

He shakes his head. "No…" He begins but Gunnar cuts across him.

"As a wedding gift from our family to yours we have booked you the honeymoon suite at the Astoria."

My eyes connect with his as I take in the words. "What?" I half snap.

"Come now, Preston." Levi says. "Surely you want this wedding to get off to a good start? Afterall, my niece is used to the finer things in life, I expect you to treat her with respect."

Like they have up until now? They've already stated how much they want me to fuck her brains out. Hardly the words of a respectful family.

It feels like the room tenses.

I can't read the expression on Nico's face as he side eyes me. "The honeymoon suite?" I say acting like I'm suddenly honoured.

Beside me Ruby looks like she's crying again. God, this is fucking awful.

My anger spikes and before I can stop myself I'm on my feet. Levi looks at me like he wants this fight, like this was the entire point of today's proceedings.

My eyes drop to Ruby. She's huddled up like she just wants to disappear entirely and I can't say I blame her.

"Fine." I growl back. If they want to play this game, then I'll meet them head on. I grab Ruby's arm hauling her to her feet more roughly than I mean and she lets out a yelp. "Enjoy the rest of the party." I say before leading her out to what feels like a frat house round of applause.

Grab your copy here:
https://www.amazon.com/dp/B0CM7MSP5S/

OTHER BOOKS

by

Ellie Sanders

Twisted Love Series – A dark, Romeo & Juliet retelling.
Downfall
Uprising
Reckoning

The Fae Girl Series
A Place of Smoke & Shadows
A Place of Truth & Lies
A Place of Sorcery & Betrayal
A Place of Rage & Ruin
A Place of Crowns & Chains

A Mafia Romance Series
Vendetta: A Mafia Romance
Coercion: An Age Gap Mafia Romance

Sexy Standalones
Good Girl: A Taboo Love Story

ABOUT THE AUTHOR

Ellie Sanders lives in rural Hampshire, in the U.K. with her partner and two troublesome dogs.

She has a BA Hons degree in English and American Literature with Creative Writing and enjoys spending her time, when not endlessly writing, exploring the countryside around her home.

She is best known for her romance / fantasy novels 'The Fae Girl' Series but has also published a series of spy erotica novels called 'The BlackWater Series'.

For updates including new books please follow her Instagram and Twitter @hotsteamywriter

Authors Note

The Medusa myth has been something I've been obsessed with from a really young age. I wanted to rewrite her story, to give her a sense of justice almost and for my own self-indulgence, to give her a man really worthy of her too.

I hope you enjoyed this story. It's not a retelling as such, more of my artistic twist on the tale.

I want to thank all my readers, supporters, and friends who've helped get me to this point, where I'm confident enough to write something without my imposter syndrome taking over and destroying it. I truly couldn't do this without you and your support really does mean the world to me.

I'd like to thank my editor / proofreader for once again rising to the challenge and correcting some of my truly terrible grammar errors without comment or judgement.

Thank you to my family, and especially my partner, who still hasn't gotten his head around all of this, and yet supports me with it anyway.

As always, if you liked this book, please leave a review. They really are the thing that feeds us as an author and (sadly) at times can be the difference between failure and success. If you're not already following me on social media, then why not jump on board @hotsteamywriter. I'm mostly on insta and try to engage and respond as much as I possibly can.

Made in United States
Orlando, FL
11 January 2025

57201618R00143